A HIP-HOP LOVE IN JERSEY CITY

TREASURE BEE

A Hip-Hop Love in Jersey City

Copyright © 2019 by Treasure Bee
Published by Shan Presents
www.shanpresents.com

All rights reserved. No part of this book may be used or reproduced in any form or by any means electronic or mechanical, including photocopying, recording, or by information storage and retrieval system, without the written permission from the publisher and writer, except brief quotes used in reviews.

This is a work of fiction. Any references or similarities to actual events, real people, living or dead, or to the real locals intended to give the novel a sense of reality. Any similarity in other names, characters, places, and incidents are entirely coincidental.

SUBSCRIBE

Text Shan to 22828 to stay up to date with new releases, sneak peeks, contest, and more....

SUBMISSIONS

To submit your manuscript to Shan Presents, please send the first three chapters and synopsis to submissions@shanpresents.com

SYNOPSIS

The music industry can be as cruel as the streets and nobody knows this more than sisters Kiyan and Akacia. Their father Omere was a music producer and owned one of the most popular record labels in the world. The girls grew up around music and had talent of their own. Being raped within the walls of her father's studio causes Kiyan to never want to sing again. Instead she falls in love with a young thug named Rome. He becomes everything to her and, although her father doesn't approve, Kiyan is willing to risk it all for the man she loves.

Akacia is bitter and mad at the world. She feels as though her father has never loved her the way he loves her little sister. Akacia is the wild child and lives her life on the edge doing who and what she wants. She leads a life completely opposite of her sister. Drugs, sex, men and money rule her world. She's not afraid of anything and feels she has nothing to lose. Will Akacia wake up before it's too late or will her lifestyle take her to the point of no return?

Quasiem Shakur is sexy, dangerous and paid. He hasn't always had the best life. With no family, and only the support of his two best friends, Qua is on a mission to get rich quick. He loves music but fast money is all he knows. Qua put his dreams of music on the back burner to live out his dope boy reality. He lives by the rule 'Love will get you killed' until he lays eyes on Kiyan. All of a sudden, love doesn't seem so bad, and Qua is willing to do anything to keep her by his side.

In this story of love and hip-hop, nothing is what it seems. Nobody is who they say they are and the twist and turns will keep you on the edge of your seat until the very end.

Chapter One
KIYAN 'YANNI' MAJORS

"Baby, I love you so much." I said to Rome. He smiled at me showing them pearly white teeth against his midnight black skin. I always loved when he smiled because most of the time, he wore a mug on his damn face, frowning at everything. So, in these moments when I got to see my thug smiling and being carefree were everything to me.

"I need to get you home before ya bitch ass Daddy start blowing you up." He said.

"One, don't talk about my Daddy, and two, my phone is off, and I don't care about getting in trouble or none of that other shit. I just wanna be with you." I told him honestly.

I was 18 years old, had just graduated from high school and my Daddy was so overprotective the shit wasn't even funny. He was a music producer who had eventually opened his own label and some of the most talented artists in the world were signed under him. He was a boss. Me and my sister grew up in the industry and to me the streets were safer than the studio any day. So much bullshit had happened to me in that damn industry that even though I could sing my ass off, I never would. Couldn't ever see myself being a part of something so fuckin wicked.

"That ya word?" He said to me. Eyes low from all the loud he had smoked. I moved from the side of the couch I was sitting on and straddled him, kissing his neck and then his lips.

"You better go head before you start some shit you can't finish Bae." He whispered in my ear before accepting my tongue into his mouth. We kissed with so much passion. I wanted him so bad. My Daddy didn't approve of this, of us. He said Rome was from the gutta and not good enough for his baby girl, but what he didn't know was that Rome was too good for me. He knew every secret, every embarrassing soul shattering thing that had ever happened to me and he loved it all. He made me laugh when I wanted to cry and he had the ability to piss me off for the smallest shit. No matter how much I loved my Daddy, I would leave it all behind to live in this one bedroom apartment with my nigga.

"I want it." I moaned in his ear as I grinded my pussy into

his hard dick. I could feel it pulsating under the grey Nike sweatpants he wore.

"You sure, you know you ain't gotta do shit you don't wanna do; a nigga want the pussy bad, but I can wait for it." He said but he didn't really wanna say it. He just had to let me know that he always had my best interest at heart. I wasn't a virgin, but I had never done this before if that made sense and for the last year, I had been keeping the cookie in the cookie jar. Rome was so patient and never got bored with me despite the lack of sex; he was my fuckin rider period.

"Yes, now quit playing and give me the dick." He stood up so fast with my legs wrapped around his waist and carried me to his bedroom. He laid me down on the bed and removed my clothes. I stared at him intently as he stripped. I could never get enough of looking at this nigga. He stared at my pussy admiring it for a few seconds before he took my clit in his mouth and made me arch my back. He spelled his name in my pussy repeatedly, sucking on my clit hard, then licking it softly before he stuck his tongue so far inside of me that his nose tickled my clit causing me to come hard. He licked it all up as my legs shook uncontrollably. He kissed his way up until his lips were on mine and I was tasting my own juices. I could feel his dick rock hard at the entrance of my pussy.

"I'm sure." I said because I knew his ass was getting ready to ask me that. He entered me slowly and I tensed up.

"You gotta relax bae. Let a nigga in." He said before kissing my neck. His lips on me was always magic. I did what I was told and relaxed; he placed kisses from my lips down to my breasts and back again. He worked his way all the way inside of me and the more I let him take control of my body the better it felt.

"Ummm baby." I moaned.

"That's right, give me my pussy." I don't know what he was doing to me, but it felt so damn good. My legs were shaking, and my pussy was so wet. I looked up into the face of the man of my dreams, and he was biting his bottom lip and looking so sexy while he fucked me into oblivion.

"Damn bae." He sexily moaned in my ear. Right then it was like an outer body experience. I was tingly all over and my pussy gushed with juices as I came all over him.

"Rome! Rome." He looked in my eyes, then bit down on his bottom lip again before cumming deep inside of me. Finally, sex and pleasure had joined forces in my mind. The reason I was so scared to have sex with Rome in the first place was out of fear that I wouldn't enjoy it, but I was wrong. I wanted nothing more than to sit on his dick forever after this. He laid next to me and pulled me in his arms.

"You know I love you right." He asked me, my eyes were heavy, and I was drained of all energy.

"I know and I love you too. You're the best thing that ever happened to me."

"Promise me that if for some reason we don't work out that you'll never let a nigga take advantage of you again. You ain't weak bae."

"There will never be another nigga Rome." I promised.

"I might not always be here Yanni. Just remember if something happens that this is real. Me and you are as real as any love can get." He said.

"Stop talking like that." I said and he chuckled.

"Ok, but one more thing. If we ever have a daughter name her Italy."

"Why Italy?"

"Rome is the capitol of Italy."

"I'mma give you a bunch of black ass babies and name them whatever you want baby. I promise."

$$

For the next three days, I kept my phone off and ignored the world. I knew my Daddy was going crazy looking for me but this time with my baby was all that mattered. We stayed up all night talking and then we fucked each other to sleep only to get up a few hours later and do it all over again. I loved waking up next to him every morning and going to sleep in his arms. Finally, I turned my phone on, it was 5am and me and Rome had just finished having sex once again. Once the phone came completely on, I noticed I had about 150 text messages. Most from my Daddy and a few from my sister Kaycie and best friend Quinn. Rome looked over my shoulder and kissed the side of my neck.

"Come on, Princess; let me take you home for ya Daddy put out a missing person report or some shit." He said. I pouted.

"I don't wanna leave."

"But you must. Don't worry I'll see you later. I'll pick you up after I bust a few moves. I don't give a fuck what ya Daddy say. I'm coming for you, but you need to handle this shit." I turned to face him and kissed his lips.

"You ain't bout to get rid of me without giving me at least one more round."

"I done turned ya sexy ass out." He said as he slapped my ass. He roughly grabbed my neck bending me over and entered me from the back.

Finally, after we had showered, we were leaving out of the house for the first time in three days. We held hands and when we got to his car, he grabbed my waist stopping me from opening my own door so he could open it. I turned around and hugged him tight.

"I love you." I said for like the millionth time.

"I love you more Bae." He said. I kissed him and got in the car as he closed my door and went around to the driver's side. Suddenly right as he opened the car door, I heard tires screech and gun shots.

"Noooooooo!" I yelled as I watched bullet after bullet enter him. He leaned up against the open door and I grabbed him by his waist and struggled to pull him inside. Finally, his body hit the seat and his head fell into my lap. There was blood everywhere. His eyes were open, and his beautiful face was covered in blood while he struggled to breathe.

"Rome please baby, please get up. Don't do this to me, not right now. I need you so much baby, come on."

"Yanni.......love....you."

"Shhh, don't try to talk baby. I hear sirens; help is coming. Please just hold on. Don't leave me. I love you so much."

His eyes fluttered as he tried hard to keep them on me. He squeezed my hand hard with all the strength he had left and then with a small smile on his face he was gone.

I didn't care about the blood. I cradled him in my arms and kissed his lips, his blood staining mine. I could taste it. Life spilled out of him and I sat there praying and wishing that God would just give him back to me. When the cops and paramedics got there, they tried to get me to let him go but I wouldn't; he wouldn't want me to. I held him in my arms and talked to him, told him how much I loved him and how our plans for a life together had been cut short way too soon. One of the cops took my cell from my bag that was sitting on the floor and answered it. My Daddy had been calling nonstop since I turned my phone on that morning. After about 20 minutes my Daddy was standing by the passenger side door.

"You have to let him go baby girl so they can take care of him." He said.

"I can't Daddy. He wouldn't want me to leave him."

"You were here with him til the end and that's what important to him that he didn't go alone."

"He's only 20 Daddy. We have our whole lives to be

together." I was in shock. I couldn't for nothing wrap my mind around this shit. Finally, one final kiss on his lips and I let go. Let my Daddy carry me in his arms to the car and within a half hour I was home still covered in blood laying in my bed. The tears came so quickly I thought that I would drown myself.

"You have to clean all that blood off of you."

"Not right now Daddy; it's all I have of him."

Two Days Later...

I laid in bed clutching the Ziplock bag that held my bloody dress. I know it was crazy, but I hadn't been able to let that dress out of my sight. I went over and over in my mind replaying the conversations we had over those three days. He was talking crazy almost like he knew something would happen.

"Baby take this key. Nobody knows about this spot but you. Everything in here is yours, remember that." He said.

"I already bought you a ring. Just waiting til the right time to get on one knee and make you my wife." I remembered him saying.

I got out of bed and grabbed his key along with my car key and went to the apartment. I started looking around going in all the closets and draws before I started filling a garbage bag with the stuff I wanted. I took his pillows because they still smelled like him. I took the shoebox of pictures he had and his jewelry. I opened the nightstand and that's when I saw the ring box. I opened it and saw the most gorgeous three carat diamond ring. It was the same one I tried on at Tiffany's when we were in the mall one day; he remembered.

I cried hard for a love lost. I stuck the ring in my pocketbook and continued stuffing some of his favorite clothes in the bag along with his cologne. Anything that smelled like him I took it. When I came across the safe, I opened it and it was seventy thousand dollars in it. Rome was working his way up in the game and saving so he could cop straight from the connect and cut out the middleman. I took the money before taking one last look around the apartment and left. I loaded the stuff in my trunk and drove over to his mother's house. They didn't get along, in fact he hardly ever went to see her, but I knew she would be hurt behind this. He was her baby boy and although they bumped heads a lot, they loved each other. I knocked on the door and Ms. Shannon answered. Her face was red and her eyes were puffy much like mine. She reached for me and hugged me.

"Hey Yanni. How you holding up?"

"Not good and I see you ain't doing so good either."

"Yeah, this is a hard one."

"I just wanted to give you this."

I handed her the black plastic bag I put the money in; she opened it and looked at me in shock.

"I found it at his house, and I know he would want you to have it." I said.

"You at least should take something." She looked at me in concern.

I have some of his things. I don't need the money." I said to her and hugged her. I also gave her the keys and the address in case she wanted something too of sentimental value.

"He really loved you Yanni." She said.

"I know."

Chapter Two
AKACIA 'KAYCIE' MAJORS
Two Months Later

"Yanni this, Yanni that." I yelled annoyed as I sat in the studio next to my father while he mixed beats for this rapper named Tron.

"Ya sister is going through a lot Akacia." My Daddy said to me like I was bothering his ass or something.

"It's been two months daddy. At this point she's just being dramatic. Can I just have some money? I wanna go to the mall with Stacy and Meesha." My Daddy stopped what he was doing once again. This was a 100,000-dollar session and I gave not one fuck. He handed me his black card and I kissed his cheek.

"Akacia, see if your little sister wants to go. She should really get out of the house. Pain like that doesn't go away. She needs all of us to assure her that we got her back."

That shit went in one ear and out the other. Me and Yanni were 11 months apart, but we were never close. She got on my damn nerves. She was Daddy's little girl and I was Daddy's little fuck up. She got caught with her thug ass boyfriend that Daddy had forbade her to be with, and not only that, but she was there when he was killed and yet Daddy was babying her ass as always. If it was me, he woulda took my car, tried to send me to boarding school and the whole nine but not his Princess Kiyan. I pulled up to Stacy's house in the heart of the hood blasting Trina's "Look Back at Me". I loved the attention I got from these niggas. A nigga named Twist walked up to my car and leaned down, so he was right in my face.

"When you gunna stop playing with a nigga Kaycie."

"What makes you think I'm playing with you." I flirted back.

"I'm tryna see what the pussy feels like." He said getting straight to the point.

"Nah, I'm tryna let Qua see what the pussy feels like." I said looking past him and across the street at Qua as he leaned up against his Mercedes truck. Twist laughed and waved me off.

"That nigga ain't thinking about you."

"Says who?" I challenged.

"Aye Qua she tryna give you the pussy." Twist yelled across the street.

"Nah, that's all you fam." He replied. They all started laughing as Twist made his way back across the street. By the time Stacy brung her ass out of the house, I was pissed. I didn't even let her get all the way in the car before I sped off down the street. Qua's ass was forever acting funny but he better humble himself. They treated him like a Boss in the hood, but he worked for my Daddy so in reality I was his fuckin Boss. Bitch ass, fine ass nigga. I rolled my eyes.

"Girl, what the fuck is wrong with yo ass?"

"Nothing, I'm straight. I wanted to go get Meesha and go to the mall, but Kev want us to come fuck with him. You down?"

She rolled her eyes at me this time.

"I guess if he still paying to play. I don't like that old ass nigga like you do so anytime he in this pussy it ain't free." She said.

"He got you." I assured her before driving to the hotel I told him to meet us at. Kev's ass was a freak and I liked that about him. He loved to see me eating Stacy's pussy and I loved to turn him on. Stacy was always fronting like the dick wasn't good and she wasn't into girls, but I couldn't tell the way the bitch was always squirting when the three of us were together. She loved it just as much as I did. Five hours later, Kev was paying Stacey for her services and I sent her on her way so I could spend some alone time with him.

"How Yanni doing?" He asked causing me to dramatically roll my eyes.

"The hell if I know. Why the fuck you asking me about Yanni anyway?"

"Damn, she went through some traumatizing shit. I'm just asking."

,;[]\'}{;.p¬;/"Well I don't know so don't fuckin ask me." I said. Kev was a big, husky nigga, brown skin with a bald head and full beard. He wasn't all that cute, but something just had me drawn to him.

He walked up to me and grabbed my throat hard slamming me against the wall I was standing in front of.

"Didn't I tell you to watch ya mouth when you talking to me." He let me go and as soon as my breathing was regulated, I slapped the shit outta him.

"I keep telling you I ain't ya wife. Keep ya hands off me."

"Whatever. I got some shit to do so I'm bout to slide. I'mma keep the room; meet me back here later." He told me as he dressed and headed for the door. I laid around for another half hour before I got in the shower and headed home.

When I got to my house, I was annoyed to see my father's little sister sitting in the living room with Yanni. Yanni looked like she didn't want to be bothered as Aunt Janine talked her ear off about some bullshit.

"Hey Aunt Janine." I said being phony. She walked up to me and gave me a hug.

"Hey Kaycie. How you are?"

"I'm good. Hey Uncle Kev." I smirked at him making him uncomfortable. Yeah y'all heard right. I was fuckin my Aunt's husband and my father's right-hand man. I often thought that I didn't even like the nigga. I just liked having one up on my father and his sister. Yanni got up and headed towards my Daddy's office and that annoyed me as always. The bell rang and I walked over to get it and was greeted by Qua. He was like the son my father never had. He was the man in these streets, but he could rap his ass off. Daddy wanted him in the studio, but he was much more comfortable slanging bricks. Daddy thought I didn't know he wasn't a legit businessman like he proclaimed to be, but I knew everything about his sneaky ass.

Chapter Three
QUASIEM "QUA" SHAKUR

The block was jumping as always. I stood against my brand new 2019 BMW X3 truck. I had no reason to even be out here since I sold my shit wholesale and let my soldiers play the hand to hand shit, but the hood is all I know. A fein named Natalie walked up to me tryna cop some work.

"Quasiem you got it?" She asked avoiding eye contact with me and looking at her dirty ass hands.

"Where the money?" She pulled out a twenty-dollar bill and handed it to me.

"Aye Haz serve this bitch for me." She walked over to Haz and he served her before walking over to me.

"Bruh you cold as fuck for that shit." He said.

"You know this nigga ain't tryna hear that shit." Twist replied while putting fire to the end of a blunt he had just rolled.

The only reason these niggas was even able to speak on my personal business was because they were my brothers. Best friends since free lunches and freeze tag.

"I don't give a fuck how high that bitch get as long as she got the money to pay for the shit. No freebees over here."

They thought it was crazy of me to sell to my own mother, but I didn't give a fuck about nobody but them and they should have known that shit by now.

"Hey Qua."

I looked up to see Siena coming my way.

"Wassup."

"Why haven't I seen you?" She said with a roll of her eyes.

"What I tell you about questioning me and shit?"

"Dam Qua, I just wanna spend time with you, make you feel good. I thought we had something between us." She pouted and moved closer to me.

"We did; hard dick and wet pussy." Twist and Haz started laughing pissing Siena off even more.

"Fuck you too Qua and them bitches you call friends." She stuck out her tongue and gave us the finger before her ghetto ass walked off, fat ass switching from side to side until she disappeared inside of her building across the street.

"Siena bad as fuck bruh." Twist commented.

"You want that, you can have that my boy." I told him honestly.

"Man, Capri finna come up here and air the whole block out if you don't keep ya dick in ya pants nigga." Haz laughed.

"You damn right; she straight wildin for the dick." Twist said speaking on his crazy ass baby momma.

My phone vibrated in my pocket letting me know I had business to take care of.

"I gotta slide. I'll meet back up with y'all later to handle that sale."

"I gotta slide too. Meesha been blowing me up all fuckin morning." Haz said.

"Be safe bruh." They told me before I peeled off the block and headed to OG's house.

$$

It took me about 30 minutes to get to Livingston, NJ where OG lived. I rang the bell and his fast ass daughter Kaycie answered the door in some lil ass shorts and a cut off shirt.

"Hey Qua, I didn't know you was coming to see me today." She smirked and I ignored her walking pass her towards O's office.

Not only was she young but I would never disrespect O like that. The nigga damn near raised me. When I was a little dirty nigga out here stealing food and clothes, he kind of saved me. Made sure I was good and put me on to getting money. He didn't have any sons, so he basically taught me the game; it was because of him I didn't get locked up when I recklessly caught a body in broad daylight with witnesses. He made all that shit go away for me.

"You always acting like you don't wanna be bothered with

me. I know you like what you see." She said following me through the house.

The bitch was pretty as fuck, I can admit that, but she wasn't for me. When I got to the office, I knocked on the door and entered once O told me to come in. Inside the office was his other daughter Kiyan.

She slightly waved at me and looked to the floor before looking up at her father again. She looked so sad. I knew someone close to her had been killed but I didn't have any details on it; it wasn't any of my business.

For some reason my dick jumped; it was the same reaction I always had when I laid eyes on her but like her sister, she was off limits to me. I couldn't help but to admire how bad she was, though. She was the color of caramel; her hair was always parted down the middle and falling to her breasts. Whether she had it curly or straight it was always parted the same way. She was thick with nice hips and a fat ass and small breasts. Her eyes were brown, a shade lighter than mine, almost hazel, and she had some pretty pink lips and a cute button nose. She wasn't like her sister; she didn't rock them long annoying ass eyelashes and I don't think I had ever seen her with makeup on; she was effortlessly beautiful; didn't have to try at all.

"Daddy, I don't care what car you get me for graduation. Whatever you pick I'll love." Kiyan said and kissed O on the cheek.

Kaycie rolled her eyes.

"Well Daddy, I want a new Lexus truck."

"Kaycie, you just crashed up the 70,000-dollar car I got you for graduation not even a year ago. You will continue to use that Civic that's in the garage until you can appreciate what you have." O said to her.

"You always showing favoritism Daddy, and it's not fair. That's exactly why I'm about to move out and get my own."

The little spoiled bitch said before walking out of his office with Yanni following close behind her.

I took a seat in one of the chairs across from his desk and waited for him to speak.

"I called you here because I want you to consider signing to my label. I'm going all in with the music and getting out of the game and I want the same for you."

I love rapping and shit, but I think I loved the game more.

"I don't know about leaving the game right now. I'm scraping these niggas, hurting they pockets bad." I replied honestly.

"Well in that case if you ain't ready to go legit I want you to step up and run shit. You the only nigga I can trust to do so in my absence. Being that you like a son to me, I do wanna see you go legit, but I know how it is to love the streets even if they don't love you back. Just give it some thought."

"I got you OG."

"In the meantime, I need you to take Yanni to get a car. I would send her with Kaycie but Kaycie would fuck around and come back with a new whip for herself and nothing for baby girl. She been real down about some shit and I'm hoping a new whip will cheer her up." He said with a shake of his head.

Chapter Four
KIYAN YANNI MAJORS

"Where y'all going?" Kaycie asked popping that damn gum getting on my nerves.

"Car shopping." I answered dryly.

"Let me get dressed so I can roll." She said eager as fuck to be around Qua.

"Nah we good." I said.

"It ain't up to you now is it." She rolled her eyes.

I looked at Qua with pleading eyes. I really didn't want her ass to go. For us to be 11 months apart we weren't close at all. In fact, she down right hated me. I never knew the reason why and had spent most of my life trying to form a relationship with her but now I just didn't give a fuck.

"We good." He simply said.

Qua wasn't a man of many words and I liked that about him. At the place where I was in my life, I didn't need empty words. I yearned for the words that had meaning behind them; the one I got from Rome... the ones I would never hear him speak again. It had been two months of complete misery and although I was moving around and finally leaving my room, I didn't think I had done any healing at all. When we got to the dealership, we looked around not saying much at all until we went inside and right there on the showroom floor was a powder blue BMW 430i convertible.

"Oh my God Qua. I want it." I squealed in excitement as I ran over to the car and got inside.

"What Lil Shorty wants Lil Shorty gets." Qua said and walked off. He came back 20 minutes later with the title and keys.

"Yay! I can't wait to go get Quinn and stunt on all these bitches." I did a lil twerk and Qua laughed. "Wow he smiles." I said.

"Just get in the car so I can follow you home. I gotta bust some moves."

"I'm not going home. Thank you though for coming with me." I said to him.

"You sure you straight?" He questioned.

"If I didn't know any better, I would think you cared. As far as the hood know Quasiem Shakur don't care about nothing or nobody."

"Damn, that's how they talk about me." He chuckled. "You be safe out here Lil Shorty." He told me. He watched me drive away and I headed to Quinn's house. I hadn't seen my best friend since Rome's service, and I missed her.

I stopped at the liquor store and got us some Mike's Harder Lemonades and a bottle of Remy. I had plans on getting fucked up, trying to drown the pain and then passing out in Quinn's bed. When I pulled up, she was on the porch. The block was live, niggas on the corner, kids running around and people on their porches smoking and drinking like me and Quinn were about to do. She had on some jean shorts with a cut off shirt. The weather had finally broken after not giving us much of a spring and bitches was out here damn near naked. Quinn was light skin, skinny with big titties and the most beautiful face I had ever seen. She always kept her hair in a wrap that fell pass her shoulders almost to her breasts, she had green eyes and the niggas was always trying to get her attention.

"Look what the cat drug in." She said standing to her feet and hugging me tight.

"I missed you bitch."

"I've been worried sick about you Yanni." She said while we took a seat on her porch, and I handed her the bag with the liquor and the ice cups in it. She made us some drinks and we got comfortable in silence watching the chaos of the ghetto.

"This shit has been so hard for me Quinn."

"I know babe. I seen how y'all were with each other. How much y'all loved each other. I'm here for you every step of the way." She said causing a tear to slide down my face.

"Onna gang." I said causing us to break out in a fit of giggles.

We sat on her porch getting drunk for hours, then we heard "Cash money taking over for the 99 and the 2000."

Next thing I know it was a full twerk session on her front porch. I was bent over in my Ethika tights with the matching sports bra that showed through my damn near see through white tank, shaking my ass while Quin threw her ass in a full circle. I felt a pair of arms wrap around my waist and carry me down the stairs and out of the gate. I was too drunk to fight back so all I could do was giggle as the person placed me on my feet and turned me around. I looked at Qua and saw a little fire in his eyes.

"Shaking ass in the middle of the hood? That's what you doing now Lil Shorty? Got all these fuck ass niggas staring at you and shit."

"I'm just fuckin it up with my bestie. I ain't worried about these niggas."

"Yeah but they damn sure worried about ya lil ass."

"This the second time today you acting like you care about lil ole me."

"Let's go. We off this." For some reason I had always trusted him, so I didn't hesitate to hand over my car keys and get in the passenger seat.

"Quinn, I'mma call you tomorrow baby." I yelled out to her right before Qua sped off the block.

"What you doing in the hood this late anyway?"

"Just tryna drink away some of the pain."

"Wanna talk about it?"

I shook my head no because to talk about Rome right now literally felt like I was back in that car covered in his precious blood. When we pulled up to my house it was 1 am. I got out of the car and Qua followed behind me as I opened the door. I was going to head straight to my room when in the living room I saw a man. My father normally had his poker game on Friday nights, so I was going to ignore him until he turned around. Immediately I started to hyperventilate. My chest felt tight, my hands were suddenly sweating, and I felt like I couldn't breathe.

"Aye Lil Shorty you aight." Qua grabbed my face in both of his hands forcing me to look at him as tears spilled from my eyes. I ran into the bathroom down the hall and he was right behind me. I sat down on the toilet and put my head down on knees. Qua kneeled in front of me and grabbed my hands.

"What's the matter? Kiyan?"

Every memory came flooding back. It wasn't like they had been locked away or anything because I dealt with this shit constantly but seeing his face had me feeling like I was 12 years old again in his studio, in his car, in the bathroom and in his office. I cried hard for the little girl he violated, for the innocence he had stolen making me so afraid to give my body willingly that I had missed precious time being intimate with Rome. He sat down on the floor and pulled me into his lap. I heard Rome's voice in my head telling me that I wasn't weak. I remembered the first time I tried to have sex with Rome and how I caught a panic attack much like this one. He comforted me the same way Qua was now. He was unjudgmental as he took the burden from me and I thought it was dead and gone with him until I saw his face.

"He raped me. When I was 12, he asked my father if I could come to the studio and sing a hook for one of the artists. Back then I was always singing background, doing hooks and stuff like that because I just loved to sing so much. He was my father's friend and business partner and we had known him our whole lives. He had never looked at me wrong or made me feel uncomfortable. I loved him. So I get to the studio and I lay down the hook and then all of a sudden he tells me he needs to fix the mic. That it wasn't sounding right so he comes into the booth and he's leaning over me to fix whatever the problem was and then he kissed me on my lips.

I pulled away but he just grabbed me and kissed me again. I tried to fight him, but I ended up on the floor of the studio. He held me down, spit on my vagina and then he raped me. I can remember screaming so loud that my throat hurt even the next day. He gripped my thighs so tight while he held my legs open that they were bruised for days. There was so much blood, and when he was done with me, he put a gun in my mouth and pulled the trigger. It was empty but I didn't know that until I heard the click. He violated me for almost a year until I found out that he was doing it to Kaycie too. She got tired of it and she made a video of him having sex with her. She used it to get him to leave and I haven't seen his face since."

No sooner than I got the last word out of my mouth Qua was up on his feet and out of the bathroom. I sat there trying to get my thoughts together, feeling rejected until I heard the commotion coming from the front. I ran out of the bathroom to see what was going on and there was Qua pistol in hand beating the shit out of Johnny. He was damn near unconscious and there was blood all over the white marble floors. My Daddy came out of nowhere and attempted to pull Qua off that perverted bastard but Qua was on a thousand. His eyes were black, and it was like he was a totally different person. Daddy finally got a hold of him and Qua's breathing was hard like a raging bull. I walked over to him and grabbed his hand. Almost instantly he was back staring into my eyes making me feel something I hadn't felt since I first laid eyes on Rome.

"What the fuck is this shit about?" My Daddy barked at Qua. Qua was still heated and once he noticed Johnny struggling to get up, he pointed the gun he had in his hand right at his head.

"Say the word Lil Shorty." He told me never taking his eyes off Johnny's bloodied face. I wanted to go ahead and give him the green light, so I didn't have to worry about this nigga anymore. Daddy stepped in front of Qua and placed his hand on the gun.

"What the fuck is this about?"

"It ain't my secret to tell OG." Qua snarled.

"He raped us. When I was 12 was the first time for me but it happened countless times within that year until Kaycie taped him doing it to her and black mailed him to make him leave town." I whispered never wanting to cause my Daddy any pain. The look on his face was one of pure hate. Daddy backed away from Qua and wrapped his arms around me. No sooner than my face was buried in my Daddy's chest I heard the shot that set me free in so many ways.

Chapter Five
QUINN ISSACS

No sooner than Yanni left with Qua, my boyfriend Niko pulled up. I met him while hanging in the studio with Yanni and Kaycie. He was signed to Omere's label Major Hits and he had a beautiful voice. When we first started kicking it shit was perfect between us but somewhere along the line things had changed. We were a year in, and I was ready to end it, but my heart wouldn't allow me to do the very thing my mind knew that I should.

"Why the fuck niggas texting me telling me my bitch out here shaking her ass? You know I can't stand when you be on that dumb shit." He yelled. Grabbing me by my arm and pulling me towards the front door.

"Get off me. I was having a good time with my fuckin friend. I keep telling you, you ain't my damn Daddy." I snatched my arm away from him and walked into the house towards my room. My mother worked overnight as a nurse and my brother was locked up doing life for a double homicide.

"And I been calling ya hoe ass all day. Stop fuckin playing with me." He yelled.

"I don't give a fuck about that shit. You were calling me cuz once again I caught ya dirty dick ass being unfaithful. Who the fuck is Malaysia? And why the fuck she calling my phone talking about she pregnant by you?" I said with tears running down my face. I was beyond tired of his bullshit.

"I don't know no fuckin Malaysia." He said with a straight face.

"Just get the fuck outta my house Dominick. I'm done with you and ya bullshit. I can have any nigga I want. I'm not about to keep letting you treat me like shit." I turned around to walk out of the room when he slapped the shit out of me.

This was another reason I needed to leave Niko; he was forever putting his damn hands on me. I fell into the door and he grabbed me by my neck and banged my head repeatedly against the door. I was feeling dizzy. I tried to push him off me, but he wasn't letting up. I was seeing double by the time he finally let me go. My head was pounding, so I reached my hand up and touched the back of my head and when I saw the blood all I could do was cry. He was yelling and ranting but I couldn't even concentrate on what the fuck he was talking about. I was just so sick of all this shit. He had been begging me to move in with him, but I refused because I couldn't trust him and his temper. If he got me alone, he would probably kill me.

He sat on my bed and lit a blunt, smoking without a care in the world while I laid on the floor in pain. I finally got the strength to get up and go into the bathroom. I looked in the mirror and was disappointed in the weak bitch that I saw in front of me. There was a big red handprint on the side of my face and my hair was soaked in blood. I turned on the shower and stepped in grabbing the Shea Moisture Shampoo. I washed my hair as much as I could. I had a big knot in the back of my head that made it impossible for me to wash it how I wanted. When I stepped out of the shower, I popped a Perc so that I could cope with this bullshit. When I entered my room, I rolled my eyes at the fact that Niko was still there. He had gotten comfortable and that pissed me off even more.

"Niko you need to leave."

"Baby, you know I didn't mean to hit you, but you know what the fuck is going to happen when you bring up another nigga in my presence."

"It's not about the fact that I mentioned a nigga. We both know that you've beat my ass for less and I just can't do this shit no more. The cheating, the beatings, the possible baby on the way. I'm only 18. I shouldn't be dealing with this dumb shit." I desperately tried to get him to understand where I was coming from. I hadn't thought of my relationship with Niko as toxic until I saw the way Rome loved Yanni. He treated her like glass; he was so careful with her heart. He loved her so deeply and although she had lost him, I'm glad she got to experience that type of love because any nigga that came after Rome would have some big shoes to fill. I just wish that I could be loved the way I love. Niko walked up to me and wrapped his arms around me, but I wasn't moved. This sour patch kid ass nigga was always sweet after being a sour piece of shit.

$$

I hadn't seen Yanni in three weeks. We both were going through our own bullshit but when she called me waking me up at seven in the morning I came running. I pulled up to her house about an hour later and she was waiting for me at the door. She damn near dragged me up to her room and closed the door.

"Did you get it?" She asked.

I pulled the pregnancy test out of my bag and handed it to her. She walked into her bathroom with me hot on her heels. I sat on the sink reading the directions while she peed on the stick. After she was done, she put the cap on it and sat it on the counter. She washed her hands nervously as I waited to see what the test would say. I had no idea what was going through her head, but I was wishing that the test was positive. I thought Rome leaving her a piece of him behind was something beautiful and I wanted her to have that. Finally, she picked up the test and read the results. She looked shocked and her silence was killing me. I snatched it out of her hand and read the word PREGNANT.

"What you wanna do?" I asked her.

"I don't even know. I'm so shocked right now. I can't believe this shit."

"I think you should keep it friend. It's not too often that people get miracles like this one. Rome made sure to leave you a piece of him, and I think that's dope." I said being the hopeless romantic that I was.

"You're right but should I tell Qua? We been getting close

lately and I'm supposed to meet up with him later. I feel guilty as fuck to even be friends with a nigga so soon after Rome, but he makes me feel good. I'm not crying when he's around; he makes this better." She said.

"You don't have to tell him shit and Rome would want you to move on Yanni."

Chapter Six

HASSAN 'HAZ' SHAHID

"Where you going Haz?" Meesha asked me as I got ready to go handle business.

"To work." I told her.

"You gotta get all designer down just to go Trap." She said

referring to the white Versace T-shirt, blue Robin jeans and Louboutin sneakers I had on.

I laughed at her dumb ass because no matter what I did she thought I was cheating.

"Gotta look like money to make money baby." I calmly responded.

"Look I know you think I'm nagging you and shit all the time but I just wanna spend some time with you baby."

"You don't wanna spend time Meesha. You want me laying around this bitch under you all day and that's broke nigga shit. How the fuck I'mma get to the bag if I'm in ya pussy all day long. I keep telling you to get ya GED so maybe you can take some college classes or some shit, get a fuckin job or something that will keep you busy." I told her.

As always me mentioning her doing something with her life pissed her the fuck off. She rolled her eyes and crossed her arms across her chest.

"What the fuck do I have to get a job for? You my man and been my man for three years now. You should want to take care of me." She yelled.

"I have no problem with taking care of you but all you wanna do is sit on ya lazy ass, chase behind Kaycie bird ass and spend my money. If you don't wanna get a job take ya fuckin ass to school. I need more than some pussy from you, and I keep telling you that shit."

"You stay acting like you better than me. You a drug dealer Hassan let's not forget that shit. Just because you papered up don't make you an upstanding citizen. You want me to do shit with my life that you ain't even doing with yours. The same way I run the streets, you run the streets."

"Bitch, I don't run the streets. I'm out here getting money. I want you to be better than what you are but if that's too much to ask Meesha fuck it. I'm out. I'll be back when

I'm back." I said to her and headed towards the front of our three-bedroom apartment.

"Wait Haz I don't want you leaving out all mad at me and shit. Shit hasn't been right with us lately and I don't know what to do about it. You know I love you baby."

It was funny that the bitch was saying she didn't know what to do about it when I had just told her the problem and what she could do to fix the shit. I had been with Meesha for three years. She was bad with dark skin, a fat ass and long, curly hair that I never got to see because her ass wore so much weave. At first shit was cool between us but as I got deeper in the game, I became more ambitious. I didn't wanna do this shit forever and was stacking money to give us a better life. The problem was while I wanted better Meesha was content with what I gave her. The bitch had no drive; she didn't want to do shit with herself and that was a turn-off. I loved her; she had some good pussy and some fye head but now that I was becoming a boss, she was just a bum and that shit was a turn off. Not wanting to argue with her anymore I kissed her on her lips and left out of the house.

$$

When I got home it was three am and a nigga was tired as shit. I walked into the bedroom ready to shower and get some sleep but Meesha was in the bed ass naked, legs wide playing with her pussy. Her dark skin was so smooth and perfect to me. Everything about her was physically perfect; if only I could get the mental to match. I stood against the doorway watching her rub her clit in a circular motion. I could see her pussy glistening with her juices. Her breathing got heavy and she moved her fingers faster over her clit until she shut her legs tight and moaned loudly letting me know that she had cum.

"This why you were getting on my fuckin nerves earlier? You coulda just asked me for some dick." I said causing her to jump.

She looked embarrassed and I was sure that if she was lighter her ass would be red.

"I didn't think you would be home anytime soon." She said nervously.

I took my clothes off and held my hard dick in my hand stroking it until Meesha came over to me and put it in her mouth. She sucked on the head nice and slow getting it sloppy wet before she took all of me inside of her mouth. She gripped my balls with one hand massaging them while she sucked me like a porn star. This part of our relationship was perfect and probably why we stayed together so long even though shit wasn't working. Good sex will keep you in a dysfunctional situation for years. I pulled her up not wanting to nut in her mouth because I knew her ass would try to kiss me. I don't give a fuck if it was my nut or not. I ain't wanna taste that shit; that was some gay ass shit. She wrapped her legs around my waist, and I laid her on the bed climbing on top of her an entering her slippery wet pussy.

"Damn Haz." She moaned.

I took her left breast in my mouth and then the right sucking on them until she screamed my name. I pulled my dick out of her and bent down to suck on her clit making her cum in my mouth.

"Hassan! Yes."

"Turn that ass around." She did what she was told and got on all fours with her back arched and her ass in the air.

I slapped her hard on the ass and then kissed the spot that I hit. I grabbed her by her waist and entered her roughly causing her to yell out. I fucked her hard. She tried to run from me, but I grabbed her waist tighter and assaulted her pussy. I was punishing her without slapping the shit outta her. I felt her cum again as her juices ran down my balls.

"You like that rough shit huh?" I said to her slapping her ass again.

"Yes, baby I love it." She moaned out.

I fucked her in that position for a good 30 minutes before I pulled out and came on her back. We fucked again in the shower before washing up. By the time our heads hit the pillow the sun was trying to come up.

"Baby, I'm going to go to get my GED and try to do some positive things in my life. You've done a lot for me and I want to do something to make you happy." She said surprising the fuck outta me.

"I'm not tryna force you into shit Mesh. I just want what's best for you." I said.

"Speaking of what's best for me. I want another baby."

That was a subject that she knew damn well I didn't like to talk about so instead of arguing with her I just kept my answer simple.

"We'll cross that bridge when we get to it."

The next morning, I woke up to the smell of food and Pine Sol. I guess the good dick I gave Meesha last night knocked some sense into her lazy ass.

"Good morning baby." She said kissing my lips.

"Good morning. What's all this about?" I asked her.

"Nothing. I heard what you said yesterday and I'm listening baby. Shit has been hard but I'm willing to try if you are." She said.

I had to see it to believe it but I wasn't the type of nigga to knock the effort she was putting in. I grabbed her by her waist and kissed her lips.

Chapter Seven
AKACIA 'KAYCIE' MAJORS

I was in the studio as a favor to Niko. He wanted me to sing on this track called "Juicy Love". It was no secret that me and my sister both could sing but after being raped by one of my father's business partners, she never sang again. Me on the other hand I loved it and wasn't bout to give it up for a perv like Johnny.

Ooh baby I can't wait to feel your hands all over my body;
Got my head in the clouds the way you be loving all up on me;
She leakin, drippin, pulsating boy you make my love so juicy.

I sang the hook as I swayed my hips to the beat looking Niko right in the eye. He was Quinn's nigga, but Quinn wasn't my friend. I wanted the nigga bad but up until now I had never gotten him alone. Right now, Niko was just hood famous but once he dropped this album, he was going to blow the fuck up. The words to the song had my pussy dripping and I was eager to sit it right on his face. I came out of the booth and sat next to Niko.

"One take shawty." He said handing me the Patron he was sipping on.

"Damn right so where ya bitch at tonight?"

"Last I checked, she was at ya house with Yanni." He said while playing back his vocals along with mine. He was grooving and I had to admit that the song was fire. He leaned back in his chair and I lifted the mini dress I was wearing and sat on his lap. He opened his eyes and they were sexy and low from the weed and Patron.

"I been wanting you for a long fuckin time now and I'm not about to miss out on this opportunity to have you."

"Nah. I ain't tryna get involved with none of Quinn friends. Shit already fucked up between us." He said.

"Well good cuz Quinn ain't my friend." I said before kissing his lips and then his neck. He seemed a little hesitant but once I got on my knees and freed his dick from the Jordan Craig sweats he was wearing he was all in.

My mouth watered with anticipation as I sucked him like them stupid bitches was doing the cucumbers on Facebook. I deep throated him and sucked him like I knew Quinn could never. When he nutted in my mouth, I swallowed every drop. Then I got up and took off the mini t-shirt dress I was wearing. Niko stripped in no time; he was eager as fuck to get this good pussy. I stood in front of him as naked as the day I was born while he stared at me holding his hard, fat dick in his hand, stroking it slowly making my juices flow.

"How you want it Daddy?" I seductively asked while rubbing my clit with two fingers.

"Bend that ass over."

I turned around hands planted on the sofa and tooted my ass up in the air. He wasted no time sliding deep inside of me.

"Damn Niko." I moaned. He wasn't that long, but he was fat and stretching me to capacity. And hitting my spot at the same time. No wonder Quinn's dumb ass stayed with him even after he kept beating her ass.

"Throw that pussy back at me." He grunted and slapped me on the ass.

I twerked all over that dick until I was cumming hard. He gripped my waist and stroked me hard, it hurt so good.

"Yes Niko. I'm going to cum again baby." I cried out. I wasn't really one to talk and act a fool during sex, but this nigga had me going out of my mind. It felt so good. Niko finally came deep in my pussy and the pressure from his hot cum entering me had me cumming again. I collapsed on the couch, panting trying to catch my breath while he went into the bathroom and cleaned himself off before coming back into the room and redressing. I walked over to him and put my arms around his neck kissing his lips.

"This can't be the last time I get this dick." I said to him as he gripped my ass.

"Chill before I have this dick buried in you again. I gotta finish this track." He pulled away from me.

"Well, will I see you tonight?"

"Most definitely." He replied.

$$

It had been a month since I fucked Niko in the studio and that nigga hadn't even tried to get in contact with me. I planned to fuck the shit outta him and have him chasing me, but the nigga flipped the script on me. He had the best dick I ever had, and I wanted him to myself. I had even been by the studio looking for him, but he wasn't there. Shit was sad and not even like me.

I was sitting in the living room watching TV when Yanni and Quinn walked in carrying bags. They were headed up to her room and since I was pissed about Niko, I wanted to be messy. When I walked in her room, they were both seated on the pink love seat she had in there. I sat on the window seat and folded my legs under me. They both looked at me like I had two heads, but that wasn't surprising. I didn't fuck with neither one of them bitches and they knew the shit.

"What do you want Akacia?" Yanni said rolling her eyes.

"Why I gotta want something? I can't just wanna chill with my sister?" I asked.

"No, we don't chill so what you want?" I ignored her and looked at Quinn.

"So Wassup with you and Niko? Y'all good?" She looked caught off guard by the question.

"We're perfect, why?" She answered nastily.

"Damn, calm ya ass down. I'm just asking cuz I heard he fuck with that bitch Cali that work reception at the studio." I didn't hear that, but I couldn't stand Cali's ass. She was forever saying some smart shit and I was waiting for the opportunity to whoop her ass. I knew she was cool with my sister and Quinn always kissing their ass when they came to the studio for Daddy or Niko and I knew this would start some shit between them.

"What?" She replied sounding like I had hurt her feelings.

"Yeah girl. I heard he fucked her last month at the studio."

"Well, he's performing at the BET Awards pre-show and I'll be on his arm not Cali so I ain't even worried." She said but I could see right through that façade. She was hurt, therefore my work was done, so I left out of the room with a smile on my face. On my way out the room I discreetly took her car keys off her dresser.

When I pulled up in front of Stacy's house a few hours later me and Meesha sat out front waiting on her until Qua came and knocked on the window. I had the top up and the windows were tinted so I know his ass probably thought I was Yanni. I rolled down the window with a smile on my face and when he saw me, I peeped the annoyance.

"Hey Daddy." I smiled at him.

"My bad. I thought you was Yanni."

"And what you looking for Yanni for?" I asked. The rude bastard didn't even answer me; he just walked away. I hated that the nigga never noticed me. I had always wanted him but now that I knew he had his eyes on Yanni I wanted him more.

Stacy came out and I met her on the porch with a couple bags of weed.

"What you doing with Yanni car?" She asked.

"Fuck that hoe." I said, she laughed.

"Anyway, I heard the song you did with Niko. That shit

fire but he ain't even put ya name on it or nothing." Meesha said and that shit pissed me the fuck off.

"Where you heard it at?"

"He posted the shit on all his social media pages."

I pulled out my phone and went to Facebook and sure enough he posted the shit without even acknowledging me. This motherfucka didn't know who he was fuckin with.

Chapter Eight
QUASIEM 'QUA' SHAKUR

"The fuck Yanni doing over here at this time of night?" Twist asked.

"That's that hoe Kaycie." I told him.

"Something wrong with that bitch, but ya ass ran across

the street when you thought it was Yanni. Ole pussy ass nigga." Haz said and they laughed.

"You got me fucked up."

"You moving like you love ole girl or some shit." Twist said.

"I don't love these hoes."

"Word on the street is that somebody put a ticket on that nigga Rome head."

Haz said.

"For what? That nigga was getting bread, but he wasn't moving like that for somebody to wanna pay to see him dead." I said.

"Well he must have fucked with the wrong nigga cuz I heard they paid 50 thousand to dead that nigga."

For some reason that information didn't sit well with me. I had just recently found out that Yanni was with Rome when the shit happened. I didn't know the nigga personally, but he was a stand-up guy. Always a real nigga, giving back to the community and shit like that. It was fucked up that he was probably killed over some jealous bullshit but that was the game. I was aware of the type of shit I was playing in and I knew it could only end up two ways for me; dead or in jail. O was offering me a way out, but I was a fuckin goon to the core and this life was the only one that I knew.

"Meet me at the spot in an hour." I said to them. I jumped in my car and drove home. By the time I changed my clothes, stole a car and drove to the spot an hour and fifteen minutes had passed.

"Always fuckin late." Twist complained.

"Shut ya ass up and get in. Y'all phones off?"

"You know this man." Haz said in his Chris Tucker impersonation.

When we pulled up to the destination, we waited a while checking out the location before we made a move.

"That nigga Mace just got his shipment today. Those dumb motherfuckas got all the dope they just copped in there with them right now. I had Key follow them niggas from the pickup spot to here." I said.

"Mace pussy ass going to wish he never crossed the grain." Haz said.

This nigga Mace use to be cool with us and shit. I gave his bum ass a job until he started feeling himself. He got down with a nigga he knew I didn't fuck with, copped some work and became the competition. I really didn't give a fuck cuz although he was making money he wasn't seeing as much as me and my niggas but then the pussy got greedy. Motherfucka had the nerve to try to hire a nigga to take me out so he could take over all my clientele and shit. He knew that I supplied 90% of the niggas that was moving weight in the tristate area and even had some niggas from the DMV area coming all this way to fuck with me. The nigga he supposedly wanted to hire to kill me was on my fuckin payroll and that one mistake was about to cost Mace his product and his life.

"Y'all ready?" I asked as we pulled the Ski Masks over our faces. I had no intention of leaving behind any witnesses but there could be a hidden camera anywhere and I didn't want to chance us being seen.

"Born ready." Haz said.

"It's never a straight yes or no with this nigga." Twist said as we all hopped out of the stolen hooptie that I took the plates off.

When I got to the door of the lil ran down house there was no need to kick it in because the shit was unlocked. These dumb niggas had a bunch of dope and couldn't even take the time to lock the fuckin door. This is what happens when you got a bunch of niggas playing drug dealer and shit. I slowly opened the door gun aimed and looked around. Just as we entered the house Mace was walking out of the back room.

POW POW.

I laid the nigga down quick. Haz came from behind me and moved into the kitchen where he fired a few shots laying down whoever was in there. Twist searched the rest of the house and came up empty. Mace must have thought he was being smart by only having him and his two brothers cooking the shit up. We quickly got a bag and loaded everything we could find in the shit. We were in and out in less than ten minutes. Easy money. We drove to the storage unit we owned and stashed the drugs until I could get the shit broken down and sold. I wasn't going to wholesale his shit because the shit I sold was much better and I wouldn't give it to my most loyal clients, but I would break that shit down and sale it to these fiends.

$$

By the time I made it home it was five in the morning and usually I was the type of nigga that loved to be alone. I didn't do the relationship shit. I fucked these hoes in the car, they crib, at hotels but I never wanted their company after. Lately I had been having Yanni on the brain. I wanted to get to know her. I wanted to spend time with her, and I even had this urge to protect her. Because of my mother I didn't trust no bitch and never would. My mother let my father cheat on her and beat her ass and ours. Me and my big brother Hakeem were closer than close. We were only two years apart, but he took care of me.

One day my father came home drunk, he whooped my mother's ass until she was unconscious, and he still had no plans of stopping until my 12-year-old brother jumped in to stop him. He beat my brother until he was bloody. I could still remember running in my mother's room to get the gun. I can still remember the punch that killed my brother. The sound of bones breaking as he beat his own son to death. I pulled the trigger, emptying the clip into that nigga. After that night losing her abusive husband and her son my mother turned to drugs and never looked back. I was never the same after that night. I carried a lot of guilt in my heart because if I would have had the balls to get the gun sooner my brother would still be alive. That night turned me cold. I didn't give a fuck about my mother, only let Haz and Twist in because they were my best friends before the shit happened and had my back after. People couldn't get into my heart or my head, so it was hard for me to understand why Yanni was in the center of my thoughts suddenly.

$$

Me: I'll be there to pick you up in an hour.
Lil Shorty: Who said I was going anywhere with you?"
Me: Stop playing with me. When I get there you better be outside or I'm coming in to get you.
Lil Shorty: Lol you got it.

I text Yanni as soon as I opened my eyes the next day. I had her lil ass on the brain heavy. An hour later I was sitting in front of her house waiting for her to come outside. After ten minutes I was at the door about to ring the bell when she came outside. She had on a pair of grey joggers that hugged her fat ass and a cut off shirt. I laughed because she was rocking the same colors as me and we both had a pair of low cool grey Retro 11s.

"Tryna match my fly?" She said to me as I opened the car door for her to get in.

"Great minds think alike." I replied.

"You miss me?" She asked.

I was noticing that since we had been kicking it more that she was getting bolder. I was rubbing off on her little ass.

"A lil something. Roll up for me." I told her handing her some weed and a wrap.

"Where are we going?"

"Nowhere in particular. I just wanna be around you today. That cool with you Lil Shorty?"

"Yeah that's cool."

I had a few stops to make before I could give her my undivided attention.

"Where you wanna eat at?"

"I want seafood." She told me.

We drove over an hour to JPs on City Island. They had the best seafood and what Lil Shorty wants she gets. We were seated right away and her greedy ass ordered damn near everything on the menu.

"There's something different about you. Every time I would see you before it's like you were always no nonsense, focused, mean even. Not beat for nothing or nobody and then out of the blue you show me this side of you." She said.

I thought about what she was saying before I answered her.

"You." I said.

"Huh?"

"You're what's different. I don't know why it happened when it did but I'm feeling you like I ain't ever felt no other female before. I know you just went through some shit but I wanna get to know you, be friends and all that bullshit." I told her honestly not really use to expressing myself; she had me feeling like a sucka.

She smiled up at me and me feeling like a bitch was worth it if I could see her smile like that every day.

"Friends is good."

"Before you get any crazy ideas this friend shit is temporary. I ain't bout to be sitting in the friend zone for years. You going to eventually give me some pussy." I told her honestly and she burst out laughing.

"You so crazy. I wasn't even thinking about friend zoning you."

"I'm just making sure we on the same page." I told her with a laugh.

I know a few weeks ago I was saying she was off limits but that was a few weeks ago. Fuck that shit now. Once I was interested in something there was nothing anybody could do to stop me from having it. I chilled with Yanni for the rest of the day before I dropped her off at home so I could go handle some business.

Chapter Nine
HASSAN 'HAZ' SHAHID
THE NEXT DAY

I sat in front of Twist house passing a blunt between us before I headed home. It was only 11 am and I had just come out, but I hadn't slept in a good 48 hours and I was tired as fuck. We had the mixtape Qua put out two years ago playing a song called 'The Trap Anthem'. The whole mixtape went hard as fuck but Qua wasn't tryna fuck with the music like that. I understood completely because I had a few songs with him on it, and I wasn't tryna do shit with the music either. I had been singing since I could remember but making fast money was my priority. I ain't have no mother, no father, no family so I had to take care of myself. Twist's three-year-old daughter Tyana came out on to the porch causing us to put the weed out. He was the only one of us that had a kid and we all had her little ass spoiled rotten.

"Hey Uncle Haz." She said kissing my cheek before she kissed Twist and sat between us.

"Wassup baby girl." I greeted her.

"Daddy, why do they call you Twist if your name is Tysean?"

I laughed; this nigga couldn't tell his three-year-old that the name was from him breaking some nigga neck in front of a bunch of people for raping his Aunt Talia. I was there when the shit happened; he twisted that nigga neck until it snapped. Shit was gruesome and niggas in the hood never forgot it.

"Mommy and Daddy use to play Twister a lot before you were born, and I always won." He said with a straight face.

"Cool." Tyana relied.

"You been giving that shit a lot of thought." I said laughing.

"Word. I knew one day her nosey ass would ask."

"I'm not a nosey ass Daddy."

"Don't say ass." He told her and she laughed.

"I'm about to slide." I said picking up Tyana and giving her a hundred-dollar bill before kissing her forehead.

"Thank you Uncle Haz. See you later."

$$

When I got home, it was still dishes in the sink from breakfast that morning. That shit pissed me off cuz all the lazy bitch had to do was load the fuckin dishwasher. I was about to enter the bedroom but stopped because a nigga was truly shocked at what the fuck I was looking at. I never put shit pass anybody, but this was some shit that I never expected. Meesha and that hoe Kaycie was in my bed in a 69-position eating each other out. By the looks of things this wasn't the first time; there was a vibrator and a plastic dick on the bed next to them. Another nigga would have joined them, but my dick would never get hard for a disloyal hoe. It was crazy because, one, the bitch was cheating but out of all the bitches in the world, she chose that bitch Kaycie when she knew how I felt about that snake ass bitch.

I watched for a few more minutes before I cleared my throat loudly causing the hoes to finally come up out the pussy for some air. Meesha had a look of shock and fear on her face when she saw me standing there. She jumped up off that bed and ran towards me while Kaycie just laid back on the pillow with her legs wide giving me a clear view of her pussy.

"Baby, it's not what it looks like. We were just having some fun; it's not that serious." Meesha said with tears running down her face.

"You sure you don't wanna join us?" Kaycie asked.

"Bitch, I wouldn't fuck you with a fake dick. Got my shit smelling like crab legs and shit you hoe ass bitch."

"Haz please, just let me explain." Meesha cried.

"Don't talk to me with that bitch stale ass pussy on ya breath. Get this bitch out my house Meesha before I kill her." I said. I went into the living room and took a seat on the couch and that's when I noticed the coke and ecstasy on the living room table.

The bitch was in here getting high and sucking on pussy. No wonder she ain't have time to clean the kitchen. I heard Meesha rushing Kaycie to get the fuck out while I busied myself by rolling a blunt. I wanted to pop those bitches but I wasn't in love with Meesha and honestly had been wanting a way out for a minute now, but being the good nigga I was I just felt obligated to be there for her and give the bitch time to get her shit together. Those birds had done me a favor and now I was finally going to be rid of Meesha's stupid ass.

Five minutes later Kaycie walked out fully dressed. She smiled at me and was getting ready to say something until I pulled my Glock from my waist and sat it on my lap. That bitch thought twice about saying some dumb shit and got the fuck out of dodge. I faced a whole blunt and a half to calm myself before I went back in the room to deal with Meesha. She had rushed and took a shower and hopefully brushed her teeth while I was in the front. She was still crying wrapped in a towel and those tears no longer moved me.

"I'mma nice nigga. At least I like to think that I am so I'mma give you until the end of the day to get ya shit and get the fuck out."

"Baby, please don't do this to me. I was high and I swear it will never happen again. We were just fuckin around having fun; it's not that serious. I love you Hassan. Please let's just work this out." She cried. She tried to grab my arm, but I pushed her back causing her to fall on to the bed.

"I can't trust you Meesha. I'm out chasing a fuckin bag and you in my house getting coked up and eating pussy. I told you to keep that sneaky ass bitch out of my house and to stay away from the bitch and in return you decided to fuck her instead." I said calmly.

"She's my friend. I don't tell you who to hang out with and

you should give me the same respect. It's not like you caught me with a nigga; it was just some harmless girl shit that's all. You know I don't have nowhere to go. Please Haz don't do this to me. I can't go back to being on the streets. You know how that shit was for me before. Please baby, I'll do whatever you want me to do, just please don't leave me." She hysterically cried.

Meesha was homeless when I met her. She was sleeping from couch to couch, stealing clothes and shit and even though she was friends with Kaycie who had a rich and famous father with unlimited resources and could have helped her she was still homeless. This was the type of shit I tried to get her to realize. That bitch wasn't ever her friend and she goes and sleep with the bitch. That was some simple ass shit. I wrapped my arms around Meesha and hugged her.

"You right Meesh; we been together for a minute now and I'm not the type of nigga that would see you homeless, so I'll leave." I pushed her off me and she continued to cry and look fuckin stupid.

"I always pay the rent six months at a time, so you got four months until it needs to be paid. I'll switch this shit and all the bills over in your name and you can have all this shit but I ain't paying ya bills and this shit between us is done. Don't call me for shit Meesha. You can either get a job or hope that ya pussy good enough to have Kaycie paying the bills up in this bitch." I told her ass before I disappeared in the kitchen to get some bags so I could take my shit.

"I love you so much Hassan. Please don't do this. You've cheated on me and I've forgiven you for that shit. Why can't you forgive me? You said you loved me."

"I never cheated on you. You just assumed that I was, and I let ya dumb ass think what you wanted. I never laid a finger on another bitch while I was with you. You think I'm some fuck nigga chasing pussy bitch. I'm chasing money and I kept telling ya dumb ass that shit. I did love you at one point but to be honest this shit is a long time coming. Being with ya bum ass is draining as fuck and I'm tired of it." I told her and continued to get all my shit.

It took me a few hours to pack everything and make sure I didn't leave shit because I had no plans on ever going back. Meesha watched me and cried the whole time but a nigga felt like a weight had been lifted from my shoulders. I rented a room at The Westin downtown Jersey City and took my shit there before I hit the block.

When I pulled up on the block, the first person I saw was Quinn's fine ass. I had been feeling her ass for a minute but never spoke on it because of the situation I was in but now that I was a free man, I knew I had to get at that.

Chapter Ten
QUINN ISSACS

After I left Yanni's house yesterday I was pissed. Niko had been doing all these romantic things and had even been keeping his hands to himself. I thought we were good but then Kaycie tells me this bullshit. I drove to his house and let myself in. When I got there, he was in the bedroom getting dressed for the day. The towel around his waist and his tattooed skin almost made me forget what I was mad about. ALMOST!

"What the fuck is this shit I hear about you fuckin Cali from the studio last month?" I yelled while throwing my bag down on the bed.

"What the fuck is you talking about? I ain't never touched that bitch or ever even wanted to." He yelled at me.

"You fuckin lying. Kaycie told me you fucked the bitch."

"Kaycie?!" He said laughing.

"Yeah nigga Kaycie."

"That bitch don't know shit about me. You better go ahead with this dumb shit before I slap the shit outta you."

"Let me go before I have to cut ya ass every way but loose up here. I done told you about threatening me and putting ya damn hands on me. I'm not having that shit no more."

"Bitch shut the fuck up. You coming in here yelling about some shit that hoe Kaycie told you. You can miss me with that shit."

"I don't know why I even try with you; I swear on everything I love I'm done so you can tell that pregnant bitch she can stop playing on my damn phone. You can have her and Cali."

A tear fell down my face and he laughed. A nigga that claims to love me was laughing at my pain.

"Shut the fuck up. That's what the fuck you get for listening to what another bitch gotta say about ya nigga. You ain't done until I tell you you're done."

Instead of arguing with him I grabbed my shit and left. I was so sick of this bullshit with him. I made it home and as always it was a bunch of fuckin people on the block. I hated living in the hood, and it would be easier for me to just move in with Niko but fuck that.

"Damn Quinn." I turned around to see Haz standing behind me. Haz was sexy as fuck with his tall ass; he was the color of caramel, with a full beard, crazy looking grey eyes and his hair was always lined up and neat like he got that shit cut every day.

"Wassup Haz. You ain't got a bunch of hoes around you today."

"I ain't never got a bunch a hoes around me. I'm too busy checking for you and being ignored on some bullshit." He said.

"You know I got a boyfriend and you got a girl." I replied.

"I'm single and you know I don't give a fuck about that nigga so let me take you out?" He said. He was so cocky and so sexy I wanted to say fuck Niko and do him how he did me, but I didn't wanna be that type of girl.

"I can't."

"I can dig that. Just let me know when you done with that pussy ass nigga."

"How you figure I'll be done any time soon?" I asked.

"You gotta get tired of crying at some point." He said and walked away.

I had no plans at all of staying home so I packed a few things before going back to Yanni's house. When I got there her car wasn't in the driveway, but I used the key I had to let myself in. As soon as I got in the house, I heard voices coming from the Den. I usually would have never eavesdropped but when I heard Niko, I got curious as to what he would be doing here. I had never seen him inside of this house. Even though he did business with O he had no reason to be here. I walked closer into the Den and my heart dropped at the words I heard.

"The nigga said he need more money." Niko said to O.

"What the fuck he mean he need more money. He knew the price I was paying to have Rome killed when he took the fuckin job so I ain't given the nigga shit else." O barked.

"He said it's getting hot; he needs to get outta dodge. Him and his brothers."

"I'll take care of it."

My heart dropped to my stomach and I felt like I would throw up. I couldn't believe Omere had anything to do with this shit. Yanni loved her father and O was aware of how she felt about Rome. He didn't approve but that was regular shit that could have been worked out; he didn't have to kill him. I couldn't look Yanni in the face after what I had just heard so I left as quietly as I had come. I needed to think about this shit before I opened my damn mouth about this shit.

Chapter Eleven

DOMINICK NIKO MENA

Hearing that Kaycie was on that bullshit pissed me the fuck off. I fucked the bitch one time and she couldn't stop blowing up my phone. I hadn't seen or spoken to her since then and now the bitch was starting shit. I knew she was in the hood with Stacey cuz all that bitch did was post shit on Snap all damn day long. I pulled up, got out and headed straight for her. I didn't give a fuck who was out there or who saw what the fuck was about to go down. I had to show Kaycie that I didn't play games with these hoes and she wouldn't be an exception. I walked up to her and grabbed her ass by her neck, slamming her into the car that she was previously sitting on.

"Bitch, I'm not the nigga you wanna play with. I will beat ya fuckin ass hoe and I don't give a fuck who ya father is." I said to her before tossing her to the ground and heading back to my car.

The crazy bitch just got up chasing behind me laughing like some shit was funny.

"Wait Niko. I'm sorry I told Quinn's ugly ass that bullshit. I just wanted to get your attention baby. You can't fuck me that good and just ignore me after. That don't sit well with me." She said giggling leaning up against my car.

"This shit ain't no game Akacia. I'll body ya ass."

"I know and that makes my pussy wet so wassup. Can I see you later?" She asked.

This bitch was weird as fuck, but she was making my dick hard.

"I'll call you in a few."

My phone rang while getting back in the car and I was beyond annoyed to see it was that nigga Hood.

"What up?" I answered.

"Tell that nigga I need more money; it's getting hot as fuck round the way."

"You knew what the ticket was when you did the hit; 50 thousand is a good damn price for one nigga." I tried to reason with him.

"Nigga, I need to get the fuck outta dodge, me and my brother. Y'all wanted that nigga dead and I did that so tell that nigga O I need a hundred thousand dollars or shit going to get ugly around here. I ain't have not one problem bodying that nigga Rome, and I won't have a problem stepping to his ass either.

"I'll holla at him." Was all I said before ending the call and heading to O's house. I stayed at O's house for 20 minutes before I decided to pop up on Malaysia's messy ass. I let myself in with the key I had to her apartment. She was sitting in the living room eating Ice cream and watching some bullshit on Netflix.

"Why the fuck you keep calling Quinn on that bullshit."

"Because I'm due any day now and I can't even get you to answer the fuckin phone."

"I told ya ass from the beginning if you decided to keep this baby you would be doing it by ya damn self." I said to her.

"That's fucked up Niko. You would turn ya back on your own flesh and blood for some bitch that you clearly don't even love, because if you did you wouldn't be cheating on her now would you?" She said rubbing her huge stomach. All I could think about is that baby stretching her pussy out of place and that shit never gripping the same.

I didn't want no fuckin kids and she knew that shit from the beginning just like Quinn did.

"Call her phone again and I'mma stop paying the rent up in this bitch." I promised.

"I just don't understand; we were good before I got pregnant." Her dumb ass said.

"Well that should tell you the pregnancy is the problem. Come ride my dick; this probably the last time ya pussy gunna be tight anyway." I said to her.

"You sound ignorant as fuck. That don't even make no sense." She rolled her eyes.

I slapped the shit out of her for talking back. She grabbed her bloody nose and started to cry. I ignored the crying and the blood. I pushed her back on the couch and snatched her shorts and panties off before I got on top of her and entered her hard. The only good thing about pregnancy was the pregnant pussy. I fucked her while she cried and then I pulled out and nutted all over her stomach.

"Next time I tell you to do something do it. I'm tired of ya fuckin mouth. Don't call me or my girl unless you wanna be homeless bitch." I said to her and headed for the door.

I know y'all probably think I'm a foul ass nigga and I don't give a fuck. These bitches needed to learn that I wasn't the nigga to be fucked with. I gave orders and expected my orders to be followed. One of the reasons I didn't wanna fuck with Kaycie was because she was a hardheaded ass hoe and I would end up killing that bitch for playing with me.

Chapter Twelve
KIYAN 'YANNI' MAJORS
(three months later)

"26 weeks Kiyan. Do you want to know the sex of your baby?" Dr. Karon asked.

"Yes." I answered excitedly.

"It's a girl."

I couldn't help the smile that crossed my face. A little girl that I hoped looked exactly like her father. After Dr. Karon preached to me the importance on keeping up with my appointments I was done.

Sitting in my car staring at my sonogram with tears in my eyes. Rome had been gone for six whole months and God knows it was hard, but he left me Italy. I cried remembering those last moments with him; he knew that he would leave me, but he knew that I would have a piece of him to love forever. My baby wouldn't grow up with her Daddy and that was heart breaking. That pain hit me so hard and made me so angry I didn't know what to do with myself. I tried to stop myself from crying but the tears flowed freely.

"I miss you so much, I don't know if I can do this without you." I said out loud praying that he could hear me.

When I got myself together, I headed home. I was starting to show, and my baby would be here in about four months, so I needed to tell Qua and my Daddy. Me and Qua were inseparable until about a month ago. I hadn't really seen him and that was my fault because I was scared that if he knew I was pregnant he wouldn't want anything to do with me. As if he could read my mind Qua text me.

Lifesaver: What the fuck is going on with you? I ain't seen you in a few weeks and that shit got a nigga aggravated as fuck. You gunna fuck around and have me bodying niggas for nothing if I don't lay eyes on you today Kiyan.

I had him saved as Lifesaver because that's literally what he was to me. I was so deep in depression after I lost Rome that many days, I thought about ending it all so I could be with him. That was until Qua came along and gave me something worth smiling about. I laughed at his aggressive ass text before I replied.

Me: Don't be doing nothing crazy. I just been having a lot going on.
Lifesaver: Say less.

When I got to the house it was quiet which meant that Kaycie wasn't here starting no shit. I walked straight to my Daddy's office knowing that's where he would be. That's where he spent most of his time when he wasn't in the studio or at Major Hits.

"Hey Daddy." I said nervously tugging at the large T-shirt with Rome's picture on the front. For some reason I felt huge standing in front of my father. I was nervous.

"What's going on baby girl?" He replied kissing me on my forehead.

"Ok, so I don't know how to say this, so I'm just going to spit it out. I'm pregnant."

The look on Daddy's face was one of pure anger.

"It's ok. We'll schedule an abortion for the morning." He said. I wasn't expecting him to be happy about this, but I was shocked that he was being this harsh.

"I'm six months pregnant Daddy and I'm not getting an abortion."

"Your Aunt Janine and Uncle Kevon have been trying to have a baby for the longest. We can give them the baby to raise as their own. I know that would make them very happy." He said calmly like he had it all figured out.

"I'm not giving my baby up for adoption nor am I aborting her. Rome left me a piece of him and I'm keeping my baby."

"You're only 19 years old Kiyan. This is not the life I planned for you; a baby will fuck up your bright future."

"That's the problem we had when Rome was in the

picture. You can't plan my life Daddy. It's not yours to control; it's mine and I'm going to do what I think is best for me regardless of how you feel about it."

"The last time you disobeyed me you ended up in a car with a dead nigga in ya lap." He said the words so viciously I had to look at him and make sure it was still my Daddy.

I couldn't believe he was speaking on the love of my life this way.

"Wow. You didn't even know him for you to speak so disrespectfully about him. He was my daughter's father; I love him so much and any piece of him that I can get I'm going to cherish."

"I'm not raising that nigga's baby and if you decide against the adoption I will cut you off Kiyan. You won't have any money or anywhere to go. Make the right choice baby girl. Ya Daddy will never steer you wrong." I wanted to cry but I wouldn't give him the satisfaction.

I was shocked at his words; my Daddy had never been so cruel to me. I was a daddy's girl to the core. I had never known my mother. She died giving birth to me, so he was all the parent I ever had and now he was turning his back on me because I wanted to love and parent the child I created. I didn't say anything else. I went up to my room and packed my clothes, my important paperwork and anything that belonged to Rome. I made several trips from my room to my car before I finally collapsed in the driver's seat with the top down. I had nowhere to go and I was heartbroken at the way my father handled me but the way he spoke of Rome let me know that he would never lay eyes on my child. I wanted to go to the bank and take the money out of my account before my father took my name off. Just when I was about to pull off Qua pulled up next to me and got out of his car. He looked at the bags in my backseat and I could tell he was concerned.

"What's going on?" He asked. I loved his voice; it was so

deep and yet so calm. He commanded attention without doing much at all.

"I'll be ok." I said head down trying to come up with my next move.

Qua grabbed my chin making me face him. I loved his dark honey colored eyes. They looked so sexy against his deep brown skin. He had the perfect pouty lips and a cute nose. He had beautiful features, thick eyebrows, long curled lashes and one dimple that showed all the time whether he was smiling or not. He was a beautiful man, his dreads always neat and hanging just past his shoulders. For a moment I imagined myself pulling on them while his head was buried between my legs. He ran his tongue over his perfect white teeth, and I wanted to kiss him.

"Tell me wassup." He demanded.

"Got in a fight with Daddy." I said.

"One fight and you pack up ya shit." He asked.

"He wants me to give my baby up for adoption. I refused and here we are." One tear slid from my eyes just speaking my father's betrayal but also because I was nervous. I didn't know how Qua would feel about this and my feelings for him were too deep for whatever this was between us to be over.

Qua reached down and touched my stomach rubbing it through the shirt I was wearing. Italy kicked and moved around causing the both of us to laugh.

"Follow me back to my crib."

"I can't impose on you Qua. I'mma just get a room for tonight." I said not wanting him to stop touching me.

"Follow me Lil Shorty." Another command. I just smiled and did what I was told.

$$

His home was a beautiful modern style home, the outside

Grey and cherry wood. The inside was decorated in a deep burgundy, gold and navy. It was breathtaking and I could also tell that he didn't spend much time here. It smelled like lavender and vanilla and I hoped that he hadn't brought me to the house he shared with another woman.

"You live here alone?"

"Yeah."

"It smells good in here." I said with a hint of sarcasm.

"Damn, so because it smells good in here I gotta live with a bitch huh?" He asked seriously as I followed him through the house into the kitchen and took a seat at the island while he stood on the opposite side staring at me.

"No, I'm just saying it's beautiful in here; it has a woman's touch."

"I have a cleaning lady that comes once a week and as far as the woman's touch shit, an interior designer decorated the house. I told her what colors I wanted, and she made the shit happen. You hungry?"

"I'm always hungry these days. Who lives in the apartment you be taking me to."

"Ight well since you a guest and shit I'mma feed you. The apartment is mine too. I stay there most of the time. It's closer to the hood."

He took a pack of bacon out the freezer and put it in a bowl of hot water before coming back to the island with a box of pancake mix.

"Breakfast for dinner. It ain't much a nigga can cook but I can make the fuck outta some breakfast." He said making me laugh.

He mixed up the pancake batter before adding a little bit of cinnamon and some fresh blueberries. After he had his batter right, he took a griddle from under the sink and plugged it up. He placed the bacon on the griddle and then heated up a skillet with butter and started making the pancakes. After he finished, we smashed them blueberry pancakes, bacon and cheese eggs. It was so good.

"Thank you for that."

"You welcome greedy ass."

"Eating for two."

"When did you find out?" He asked while washing the dishes we had used.

"Like three months ago. I was just scared to tell you. I didn't know how you would feel about it and I was scared that you wouldn't wanna fuck with me anymore. Plus, you see how my Daddy acted."

"OG just overprotective of you that's all. I'm sure y'all will be able to figure all this shit out soon. As for me you can tell me anything. I ain't tryna come up off you no time soon and you being pregnant ain't going to change that."

"I don't know. The shit he said about Rome I don't think I can forgive."

"I feel you."

He showed me upstairs and told me I could stay in the guest room down the hall from his room. It was also decorated nicely in a turquoise and navy blue and the bathroom was right next to the room so that was a plus. I ran a nice bath and soaked my tired body. I was so excited to be a mother, but I would be lying if I said I wasn't scared out of my mind too. I never had a mother and now I would be a single mother raising a daughter without her father and I didn't know how to do that.

"Just send me a sign and let me know that you're at peace. Please just let me know that I won't fuck this up and that I'm not in this alone." I spoke hoping that some way somehow Rome could hear me.

When I got out of the bath all my stuff was in the guest room. After I dressed, I laid across the bed and watched TV. Qua knocked on the door before entering.

"I'm about to go bust a couple of moves. Nobody knows where I live except Twist and Haz and those niggas ain't coming here so you're good here. I brought all ya shit out the car because I want you to stay as long as you want. I got y'all. Text me if you need anything, I won't be back til late."

He turned to leave.

"You got us why?" I was curious to know. I didn't know exactly what we were doing but telling me I could stay as long I want and throwing around words like "I got y'all" was feeling deeper than friendship.

"I fucks with you. Why else you think I been spending all my free time with you, going on dates, shopping and shit. You even got me singing to ya lil ass and I don't even be doing no sucka ass shit like that." Qua said making me laugh.

We were down by the waterfront one day when I started singing "Trippin" by Ella Mai. This nigga surprised the shit outta me when he started singing the Jacquees version. Of course, he sounded way better than Jacquees; his voice was beautiful and had my ass ready to hop on his dick. These past few months Qua had shown me a side of him that nobody else got to see and I was falling for him harder and harder every day.

"Thank you for everything."

"I got you and her Lil Shorty. Holla if you need me. I'm out. I'll lock up."

Chapter Thirteen
QUASIEM 'QUA' SHAKUR

This having feelings for somebody was new to a nigga like me. I didn't know what the fuck to do with this shit. Caring about somebody else was a liability especially to somebody that was as deep in the streets as me. Niggas couldn't touch me and that pissed them the fuck off because there was no wife or kid for them to try to use to get to me.

Anyway, I had sold all that weak ass shit we got from Mace's bitch ass and the come up was lovely. Mace was the only competition I had on the streets and with him being a distant memory money was flowing. Siena had been blowing me up for three fuckin days now so finally I decided to bless the bitch with my presence. I knocked on her door and waited for her to answer. When she did, I walked in and took a seat on the couch. She lived in the hood, but her shit was always clean which is why I even came in here in the first place.

"Wassup Siena."

"I just miss you Qua." She was looking good in a pair of boy shorts and a white tank top that showed her hard nipples underneath.

"Oh yeah, come show me."

She removed the boy shorts followed by the tank top. I appreciated her waxed pussy and her smooth skin. Siena was a baddie. Looked like she could have been mixed with Spanish or some shit, but she didn't know who her pops was and neither did her hoe ass mama. She came over to me and straddled my lap. I took her right nipple in my mouth and my fingers found their way to her clit. I rubbed her pussy and she was wet as fuck just like I suspected. I had been fuckin with Siena on and off for over a year, but she couldn't control her fuckin feelings which is why I always had to take the dick from her. She couldn't handle it on a consistent basis.

"Umm Qua, fuck me baby."

"That ass backed the fuck up ain't you." I said with a laugh.

"Yes, cuz you ain't fuck me in a month. I need it." I kissed her between her breasts, and she humped the two fingers I had planted deep in her pussy like it was my dick. I kissed her neck and her breathing got heavier. I felt her pussy squeezing my fingers and knew she was about to cum.

"Hurry up and cum for Daddy so you can suck this dick." I whispered in her ear and then bit her ear lobe and she came hard on my fingers. I took them out of her pussy and placed them in her mouth and she sucked them clean before getting on her knees in front of me and freeing me of my jeans and boxers. She massaged my 11 inches with both hands before finally putting it in her mouth. She sucked the head hard just the way I taught her before making it real sloppy and deep throating all 11 inches.

I grabbed a hand full of her hair as I guided her up and down on my dick before she started wilding on my shit. Spitting, slurping, humming, slobbing all crazy until I busted deep in her mouth. She spit the cum back on my dick before licking it off again and swallowing it all. I handed her a magnum XL and she slid it on my dick before turning around so she could ride me from the back. I sat up and moved to the edge of the couch while she eased down on my dick. She started off slow riding me at her own pace until she felt that orgasm building and started bouncing up and down on my dick until she caught the nut she was chasing.

"Ohh Qua. You feel so good Daddy." I picked her up with my dick still inside of her and bent her over the couch. I slapped her hard on the ass to let her know to arch her fuckin back.

"Throw that pussy at me Si." She threw her pussy at me until I grabbed her waist and fucked her long and hard. She was screaming that it hurt but that pussy was squirting all over me. I gave her ass no mercy pulling her hair, slapping her ass and fucking her like I was mad at the pussy until I spilled my seeds inside of the condom. I pulled out before heading to the bathroom where I flushed the toilet and cleaned myself off with soap and hot water. When I came back Sienna was sitting on the couch like I had killed her fuckin puppy. I knew that the pussy wasn't worth the headache this bitch was about to give me. I put my clothes on and headed for the door. She stopped me like I knew she would, grabbing me by my arm.

"Why do you punish me for having feelings for you Quasiem? You come her whenever you want, fuck me all good and then get mad at me for wanting more of you." She said bottom lip quivering. At that moment I told myself this would be the last time I felt her pussy.

"I'm not punishing you for how you feel. I just don't feel the same way. You always talking about you can handle us just being cool but then you start this shit again." She rolled her eyes.

"I just want you; I fell for you even though I knew I shouldn't have and that's my fault, but you can't blame me for that. I can't help how I feel."

I pulled out a couple of hundred and handed it to her before walking out of her door and her life. I wasn't about to keep putting up with her bullshit.

When I stepped out of the building Natalie was leaned up against my car.

"I ain't got shit on me. Go up the block and holla at one of those lil niggas." I said to her without even looking at her.

"I'm ready to get clean Quasiem." She said causing me to look up at her. In her eyes I saw mine, the same shade of brown. She looked human instead of the zombie I saw any other time she came around.

"Why now? After 13 years of being a nothing ass junkie you wanna get ya shit together now?" I asked her with anger and resentment in my heart.

"I'm ready. I just need help." She said.

"I'll send Haz around here in 15 minutes. If you ain't here don't ever ask me for no fuckin help again."

"Thank you, son."

"Ya son died 13 years ago."

I called Haz and told him where she was and to take her to check in to a rehab center. I also told him to keep track of what was going on but that I didn't wanna know shit about it. I would pay for the shit and that was it. I wasn't interested in her progress and I damn sure wasn't interested in a relationship.

By the time I handled business and collected all my money and shit it was four in the morning. Yanni hadn't called me all night so when I got home, the first thing I did was check on her. She was sleeping peacefully in a pair of panties and a sports bra; her stomach was on full display and looked way bigger than it did earlier. I reached down and rubbed it and just like before Lil Mama started moving around and kicking at me. I didn't know what the fuck I was going to do but I damn sure knew that I wasn't letting Yanni out of my sight no time soon. Her young ass had done something to me that no woman had ever been able to do.

$$

I was at Major Hits meeting up with OG. He called me early this morning talking about he needed to talk to me about something important.

"Wassup. I ain't seen you in a few days." He greeted me when I entered his office.

"Chasing that bag." I replied taking a seat across from him.

"I called you here about Yanni." He said.

"What about her?"

"I saw her pull out of the driveway behind you the other day. Where is she?"

"She been staying with me."

"I can't allow you to fuck with my daughter. Bad enough she let that bitch ass nigga Rome get her pregnant. I won't allow a relationship between y'all to happen."

"Look OG, as of right now, it ain't no relationship, but I've never lied to you and I ain't going to start now. It's feelings there, we vibe together, so I'm not saying it won't get to that point." I told him honestly.

"She's too good for you. You deep as fuck in these streets and I can't allow anything to happen to my daughter."

"She definitely too good for a nigga like me. I've considered that, still considering that but if we ever crossed that line you already know I'll protect her with my life. I'll murder any nigga that even looks at her wrong." I told him.

"You're like a son to me."

"And you like a father to me."

"I don't want this to get in between our relationship." He said sternly.

"Agreed." I responded before I left out of his office. O had known me most of my life and he knew better than anybody couldn't no nigga on this earth tell me what the fuck to do.

Chapter Fourteen
QUINN ISAACS

I came home to a fuckin eviction notice on the door. I snatched it off the door and walked into the house to find my mother. This bitch was really in her room packing her shit.

"Ma why is the rent not being paid? What are you doing

with your check and the money I've been giving you?" I asked her frustrated.

"I have a lot going on Quinn and I damn sure ain't about to fight with that bitch to stay in this raggedy ass house."

"What fight Ma? All you have to do is literally pay the damn rent! What is going on with you?"

"I decided to move down south with ya Aunt Jessica. I'm tired of Jersey City and I just want a fresh start. You are more than welcome to come."

"So, you been using my money as a down payment on a new life and didn't even have the decency to tell me that shit?" I yelled at her. My mother had always been a sneaky hoe but for the most part she paid the bills and made sure I was good.

"Quinn you are grown as fuck. You can take care of ya self but right now I gotta do what I gotta do for me. We have until next week to be out of here."

I went to my room feeling defeated as fuck. I couldn't believe how selfish she was being, but she was right about one thing. I was grown. I called Yanni. I hadn't spoken to her in a few days, but I knew she wouldn't mind me staying with her for as long as I needed.

"Hey Bestie. What's going on?"

"Girl nothing much I just been going through it." She replied.

"What's the matter?" I asked concerned.

"Well for starters; It's a girl!!" She said excitedly.

"Aww Italy. I can't wait to meet my God baby." I said.

"Anyway, I told my Daddy and he started talking real disrespectful about Rome, saying how he not raising that nigga baby and the last time I disobeyed him I ended up with a dead nigga in my lap." Hearing that shit had me shocked; he had never spoken to Yanni crazy.

Always babied her and had her ass spoiled. She was a

Daddy's girl but being that I knew he had Rome killed I wasn't surprised. I wanted to tell her so bad, but I was scared to. They killed Rome and if they found out that I was going around telling people they could kill my ass too.

"He had the nerve to tell me that I need to get an abortion or give my baby up for adoption. So, I packed my shit and I've been staying with Qua." I could hear the smile in her voice.

"Qua done wifed ya ass up and you don't even know it yet." I said and her ass giggled.

"I really like him but it ain't that serious yet. I can tell he's not use to really caring about a female and all of this is new to him. Plus, I'm grieving and carrying the child of my dead lover so it ain't nothing going on but a friendship."

"Uhun, it sounds like more than fuckin friendship to me bitch."

$$

(Two months later)

Two months I had been staying with Niko, and I can truly say I never knew how evil this nigga was until I moved in with him. His ass had me terrified to even breathe too loud because I had been slapped more times than I could count since I had been there. When he was in the studio it was heaven because he stayed there for hours at a time. I wanted to suggest seeing a doctor because I swear the nigga is bipolar some days. He eat my pussy for an hour at a time, take me on dates, shower me with gifts and some days he's moody and angry and just wants to fight. I love the good days but as of lately the good days seem few and far between.

I heard his car pulling up in the driveway so I hurried my ass downstairs to the kitchen so I could warm his food and put it on the table for him. While the dinner I had cooked was warming in the microwave I got him a cold beer from the fridge and sat it on the table. By the time he walked in the door his food was hot, his drink was cold, and I was looking sexy greeting him with a kiss. I smelled the Hennessey on his breath and wanted to cry because I knew it would be a long night.

"I missed you baby." I said to him while he stared at me with cold, dark eyes.

"You sure about that?" He slurred.

"Yes baby. How was your studio session?" I said still desperately trying to play nice. I didn't feel like fighting. I had just gotten rid of the black eye he gave me last month.

He sat at the kitchen table and looked at the food strangely before taking a bite of the fried chicken breast on his plate. He ate a few more bites before he swiped the entire plate on the floor making it shatter into pieces. I jumped back moving away from him until my back was up against the refrigerator. Tears spilled from my eyes and he smiled at me. He walked up to me and kissed my lips.

"You look scared. You know I love you, don't you?" He asked me. I shook my head yes still scared that even the sound of my voice would set him off.

"Tell me you love me." He said.

"You know I love you so much baby." He kissed my neck and then removed my panties. I reached for the button on his jeans and undid it. Pulling his dick out of his boxers I stroked it slowly. He picked me up and I wrapped my legs around his waist while he slid me down onto his hard dick.

"Oooh." I moaned because although he was monster, he had some good dick and I loved fuckin his crazy ass.

He kissed me with so much passion and my pussy gushed as I came hard all over his dick.

"Damn this pussy good as fuck baby." He moaned in my ear and then bit my neck.

"And it's all yours baby."

"So, you ain't trying to leave Daddy?" He asked me still fuckin me like he hadn't just turned on the crazy switch.

I tried not to freeze. I didn't want to look guilty but now my heart was beating out of my chest and my eyes were watering just thinking about what he would do to me.

"Why you stopped? Keep giving me my pussy." He said as I continued to meet his strokes.

"I don't wanna leave you baby." I said voice cracking.

"So why the fuck you looking for apartments then?" He asked as he grabbed my throat and squeezed cutting off my air way with no real effort. He choked the shit out of me and still had the nerve to fuck me until he came inside of me. After he came, he dropped me to the floor, and I gasped for air. My throat felt like it was on fire and I tried to control my sobs because I knew that crying only excited him.

"I don't wanna leave you Niko, I swear but you leave me no choice. I don't wanna fight. I can't do this with you. I don't wanna be your punching bag." I said that shit without even thinking and instantly regretted it as soon as the word left my lips.

Before I could take it back or tell the nigga I loved him or something he had snatched me up by my hair making me stand to me feet just so he could slap me back to the floor. Blood shot out of my nose and I bit my tongue. I tried to crawl away from him, but he kicked me in the stomach not giving a fuck that he still had his Jordan's on his feet.

"Please stop, please. I'm sorry!" I screamed and backed up into the corner balling myself up in a fetal position, doing the best I could to protect my face and head.

"Bitch, I know you sorry. You real fuckin sorry." He growled at me while kicking me in my back.

"Niko! Stop!" I screamed to the top of my lungs.

"Stand the fuck up!" He yelled. "Bitch I said stand the fuck up!"

I stood up, tears and blood all over my face. He took my face in his hands and kissed my lips.

"You like when I fuck you up don't you?" I shook my head no.

"You do, you stupid ass bitch because you know exactly what the fuck is going to happen when you do dumb shit like this to piss me off don't you." Again, I didn't answer. I just shook my head while I openly sobbed. I wanted him to understand that I did love him and if he could keep his hands to himself, we would be perfect.

"I took your name off the accounts. From now on you will have access to no money unless I give it to you, do you understand?" I shook my head yes.

"I can't hear you baby?" He whispered. Kissing my cheek.

"Yes, Niko I hear you."

"I don't wanna take from you baby. I wanna give you the world Quinn but you gotta obey ya man. I need you to be submissive baby and I need to be able to go to fuckin work without having to worry about you trying to leave me." He said.

"Ok Niko, I won't leave."

"Don't worry baby. I didn't fuck up that pretty face. I know that's all you be worried about." He said like this shit was a game to him. "Go get cleaned up. I want some more of that good pussy before we go to bed."

I felt trapped and at this point I had to either get away or accept the fact that he was going to kill me.

Chapter Fifteen
AKACIA 'KAYCIE' MAJORS

I laid on my back as Kev pumped in and out of m. I wasn't participating at all. I just wasn't feeling his fat ass anymore. I wanted Niko, all of Niko. He had hit me off with the dick a few times after the first time, but that nigga loved to play hard to get. I wish he wanted me like that hoe Meesha did. Now that she lost her nigga, she thought that we were going to be some type of couple or something, but that hoe was sadly mistaken. I blocked her number and moved the fuck on with my life and she should do the same. I mean, I liked to have fun with girls occasionally, but I wasn't a lesbian and definitely wasn't tryna wife no bitch. I needed a nigga with a big dick and deep pockets.

Kev's raggedy hadn't even noticed I was silent as fuck. Didn't even give his ass the courtesy of a fake orgasm. Finally, he came and rolled his sweaty ass off me and I jumped up without even wiping my pussy and started putting my clothes on.

"What the fuck is your problem?" He yelled at me, noticing that I was tryna get the fuck up outta there.

"Uncle Kev, I just don't think this is going to work out. It's been fun though."

"Uncle Kev? You funny as fuck."

"Nigga, you are my whole Uncle, or have you forgotten." I rolled my eyes.

"Now all of a sudden you wanna end shit,. Bitch you got me fucked up." He said with his mad ass.

"Yes, it's done. I'm tired of fuckin ya old ass and honestly ever since I been fuckin this new nigga you ain't even fuckin me right. I know you just noticed I gave you pussy with no participation."

"Keep talking and I'll beat your fuckin ass in here bitch."

"Daddy, Uncle Kev raped me. He tricked me into meeting him in a hotel and forced himself on me." I faked crying and laughed at the look on his face.

"Ain't nobody going to believe that shit."

"They will when they take me to the hospital for a rape kit; ain't this ya cum rolling down my damn thigh." I rolled my eyes.

"Just get the fuck out." He yelled at me.

"Gladly. Just give me my money first."

"I ain't giving you shit hoe." He grabbed my arm and tossed me out of the hotel room on my ass and then the rude bitch threw my fuckin purse at me.

"You going to wish you never fucked with me nigga!" I screamed at him.

Once I made it to my car, I pulled out my cell phone and called my Aunt Janine.

"Yes Kaycie." She answered.

"I been fuckin ya fat ass husband for years now. If you don't believe me, he has a birth mark on the tip of his dick!" I said and hung up the phone.

She didn't do shit to me, but Uncle Kev needed to be taught a lesson. When I made it home, I wasn't surprised that my Daddy was waiting for me at the door.

"What the fuck is wrong with you?" He yelled.

"It ain't shit wrong with me. What the fuck is wrong with him fucking his 17-year-old niece and continuing to fuck me up until tonight when I broke it off with his ass." My Daddy looked disgusted by me but that was nothing new.

"I've done all I can by you. I have given you anything you have ever wanted. I have loved you unconditionally and did every single thing I can think of to keep you happy, but the shit is never enough Kaycie."

"You've done all you can by me? Right. Despite the fact that I'm not your real daughter?" I had finally gotten the courage to bring this up to him.

"What are you talking about?" He asked trying to play dumb.

"Daddy I found my original birth certificate. The one I had before you changed my last name."

"I never wanted you to find out about that. That shit doesn't mean anything to me. You are my daughter. I raised you as such and I'll continue to be your father until I take my last breath."

"You treated me different all these years. Like I was second best to your precious Kiyan and then when I was 13, I found out why. It's because you love me but not as much as you love Kiyan. Admit it Daddy. You only took me in because you felt guilty. Your daughter killed my mother in childbirth, so you had no choice but to take me in. That's not love; that's pity." It hurt to know that I didn't belong with him. I didn't belong anywhere which is why I did what I wanted to do when I wanted to do it.

"Baby girl, I never wanted you to feel that way. I love you, Akacia. I have loved you since your mother introduced me to you. You were two months old when I met you and I took on that father role immediately. You're not second-best baby; you're my first born." He said. I wanted to believe him but, on the inside, I was just so damaged.

"I want to believe that Daddy, but I don't know if I can. It's always been you and Yanni against me."

"That's not true Kaycie. I'm never against you baby. I'm on your side now and always. I'm hard on you and your sister but that's because I want the best for my girls. But if you keep on with this reckless behavior I'mma cut your ass off too." He said. I didn't like getting emotional, so I just walked away.

Finding out my father wasn't my real father was the reason I came onto to Johnny's old ass. I seduced him so I could lose my virginity. One of the only things I would ever regret is giving Johnny the green light to go after Kiyan. I told him she wanted it just like I did, but of course, when she fought him off, he quickly realized I lied. That didn't stop him from hurting her, though. It was only supposed to be a one-time thing but when she told me he had been doing it to her continuously I knew I had to stop it. My father knew what was going on with me and Johnny; he just didn't care. I wanted to hurt him by sending Johnny for Kiyan, but she never told my father until recently.

Chapter Sixteen
KIYAN 'YANNI' MAJORS

I was finally eight months pregnant and I was so excited, but I was also feeling down because I missed my Daddy. I wanted him to be a part of this journey with me, but I couldn't allow him to disrespect the father of my child. Rome would live on forever in Italy and I would never allow anyone to taint his memory. Besides me being eight months today it was also my mom's birthday. This day was also hard on Kaycie and I, so I decided to Facetime her. She answered the phone with an attitude as always, but I ignored it. Despite her face being frowned up she had her hair naturally curly which she didn't do often. She preferred it straight and was always getting it blown out. We looked a lot alike except she was a shade lighter than me and she had dark brown eyes. People always mistook us for twins, and she hated that just as much as she hated me. One day I hoped to have a close relationship with her like normal sisters, but I didn't think it would ever happen.

"What Yanni? You going to sit here staring at me all day?"

"I just called to see how you were doing. Mommy's birthday is always hard for us." I said.

"I'm good. Let me see your stomach." She said surprising me. I didn't think she cared about me being pregnant. I held the camera up so she could see my swollen belly. I was in a sports bra and tights, so it was on full display.

"You look cute Kiyan."

"Thanks, Kaycie. I just want us to get along. I want my baby girl to have a family and you and Daddy are the only family I have."

"Y'all don't understand me, Kiyan, and I'm too over everything to even try to explain."

"What's going on?" I asked genuinely concerned.

"Nothing I wanna talk about. I'm about to head into the studio now to lay down some background vocals for Tron. I'll talk to you later." She said and disconnected the call.

I don't know if this pregnancy had me emotional or if it was the fact that my family issues were really fucking with me but before I knew it, I was crying and of course Qua walked right in on it. These pass two months living together had been great. We hadn't crossed any lines except for a few kisses here and there, but the bond we shared grew deeper every day. I was grateful for the relationship we were building. He loved my baby girl as if she was his and had bought so many tiny clothes and baby stuff that I found it hilarious that his thug ass could be in the mall picking out dresses and butterfly themed blankets.

"What's the matter? Ain't no more cheese or some shit?" I rolled my eyes at his ignorant ass.

"I miss my Daddy and my evil ass sister."

"If you wanna talk to ya pops I'll take you to see him. I got ya back Lil Mama."

My nickname had upgraded from Lil Shorty to Lil Mama. Qua showed me a side of him that the streets didn't get to see. When he was behind these walls, he was relaxed, calm, funny, loving and charming. I was falling hard despite me trying to slow myself down. I felt bad because loving someone else while Rome was gone felt like betrayal, but I fully understood that I had to move on.

Qua held out his hands for me to grab so he could help me up off the couch. I grabbed ahold of him and he pulled me up. The Muslim oil he was wearing filled my nose and made my panties wet. Standing against him with his hand in mine I couldn't help but to stare into his honey colored eyes. It seemed like hours had went by when it was barely a minute and then as if he was reading my mind, he kissed me. It felt like my entire world stopped as I wrapped my arms around his neck and kissed him back. I could taste the peppermint candy and the weed on his breath, and it made me want him even more. I had no idea that anybody could kiss me the way Rome once had and as much as I hated to say it Qua's kisses were better. He had me feeling weak in the knees as we made out like there was no tomorrow. He palmed my ass and I moaned against his lips right before he pulled away.

"Lil Mama, you better chill if you don't wanna get fucked in here." I blushed red with embarrassment.

"What is this between us?" I asked him.

"You know I want you; I'm just giving you time to have my baby girl before I put this dick in ya life and make shit official." I smiled at how blunt he always was. I loved the way he was straightforward about everything.

"How you figure I'm ready to be yours." I asked.

"You already mine Lil Mama." He kissed me again and slapped me on the ass when I walked away. I went into the kitchen and started dinner while I called Quinn. I hadn't spoken to her in about two weeks but we both had a lot of shit going on.

"Hey BestFrann." I said into the phone.

"Hey Baby Mama. I miss you." She said; she sounded a little off.

"Are you ok Quinn?" I asked concerned.

"Yes, I'm fine. I'm just tired. I had to go to Cali with Niko for a show he had out there, and we got back late last night." She said.

"So, my maternity shoot is tomorrow, and I need you to be there. Bring your Calvin Klein sports bra and underwear cuz I wanna get a few pictures with you since you are Italy's God mother."

"Everybody does the Calvin Klein shit now." She said.

"Don't worry; that's just one of the looks. I'm doing a whole damn photo shoot so I'll have multiple looks." I explained.

"Ok text me the info. I'll be there."

$$

Finally, it was the day of the photo shoot and I had Qua and Quinn by my side. I was finally realizing that if they were the only family Italy and I were going to have then I was going to have to be cool with that. My first look was the Calvin Klein bra and panties. Me and Quinn took a few shots in our sports bra and jeans and then we took the jeans off and did a few shots in our bra and panties.

"I wanna do a few pictures with Daddy too in this look." My photographer Lauren said.

I was going to tell her that he wasn't the father when Qua came over to me and took his shirt off. I loved staring at his body. He was the perfect shade of smooth deep brown and his tattoos made my pussy wet. I giggled and felt my heart fill when I noticed he had on Calvin Klein boxers. I wanted to ask him to participate in the photo shoot, but I felt like I would be overstepping so I'm glad he took it upon himself to join.

We took so many cute poses that I knew for a fact that I would buy them all. I did a few more looks by myself and with Qua and Quinn and finally I was getting my body paint done. I had been itching to do body paint since I found out I was pregnant. In this photo I gave the photographer a picture of Rome and she was able to fade him out, so it looked like he was in the sky looking down on me and his baby girl. The day was a success and although I wanted my daddy and sister there sometimes things happened for a reason so I was no longer going to dwell on the things I couldn't change.

Chapter Seventeen
QUASIEM 'QUA' SHAKUR

Stepping up and taking responsibility for Yanni and baby girl was something I never expected to do, but these past few months living under the same roof as Yanni had put a lot of shit in perspective. I think I was falling in love. I had never felt this way about anybody in my life. I had a strong urge to protect her. I already knew I would send a nigga to Christ behind her because I had already killed for her. We hadn't even had sex and yet, but I was ready to move mountains for her if it would put a smile on her face.

"You ole sucka ass nigga. Missing money to do photoshoots and shit. What type of time you on my G." Haz said.

"Fuck you bitch." I replied with a laugh.

"I ain't never, ever seen you like this with no female ever." Twist said handing me the Patron.

"I know; shit is crazy. I be feeling like a bitch for real."

"You should feel like a bitch." Twist said.

"Y'all niggas better stop coming at me crazy for I body one of y'all."

"You ain't gone do shit. Ayo, on some real shit. You told me you ain't wanna hear shit about Natalie until she finished the program and she did. She came home yesterday; I got her a lil spot in the suburbs away from the hood in case you wanna go check her out." Haz said.

I can't even lie. I was surprised she went through with the rehab. I hadn't seen my mother clean in 13 years and I had never seen her carefree or even happy for that matter. Before the drugs all I saw was a weak bitch that let a nigga beat the shit out of her and her kids. I had no respect for her, but I was curious to see her. A part of me hated her and felt like I would never be able to have a relationship with her because of what happened to my brother. I didn't give a fuck about the shit I had gone through being hungry and dirty. Having to sleep on park benches and shit I didn't care about that shit, but the untimely death of my brother was unforgivable.

"I might try to check her out. I don't know."

"She been asking for you." Haz said.

We got out of the car and headed towards the strip club.

When we got to the VIP section, I ordered a bottle of Remy and Twist ordered a bottle of Patron. It had been a minute since we just kicked it, so I had plans on getting fucked up. After a while the thirsty bitches started flooding the VIP tryna make some change, but I wasn't bout to buy no pussy. I would watch them hoes shake they ass, though. A light skin bitch with a fat ass caught my attention and when she turned around, I realized it was Sienna. When she saw who was in the section her face flashed with embarrassment and she was about to walk away until I waved her over. She came over to me and stood in front of me with her hands on her thick hips. She had on a sheer black bra top and a hot pink G-string.

"What the fuck you doing working at the strip club Si?"

"I lost my job. I gotta do what I gotta do to keep a roof over my head." She said sitting next to me.

"So, you wanna be shaking ya ass for cash?" I asked her. I wouldn't want her doing some shit she didn't wanna do in order to keep a roof over her head.

"I don't have a choice Qua."

"If you really don't wanna do this shit I'll take care of the rent for a year until you get back on ya feet and I'll send somebody through tomorrow with something to keep you straight until you find a job." I told her. Yanni's little ass had a nigga going soft out this bitch.

"You mean that?" She asked.

"I'll look out for you as a friend, nothing more nothing less Sienna."

$$

three Days Later

My phone was constantly buzzing. I looked at the clock

and it was 6 am. I had just gotten to fuckin sleep after being in the streets all night, so I was pissed. I snatched the phone from the nightstand and answered it after seeing it was Sienna.

"Bitch don't make me regret giving you that bread. Why the fuck you calling me so early in the fuckin morning Si?"

"Look some nigga came in the strip club last night. He was popping big shit about how he was going to kill you and everybody you love."

I wasn't worried about none of these pussy ass niggas, so she ain't have to wake me up for that bullshit.

"Something about you killing his little brother, a nigga named Mace."

Being that I had killed Mace and his little brother Marcus Sienna could only be talking about his older brother Black. Last I heard the nigga was locked up but if he wanted a war with me I had no choice but to put his mother in another black dress.

"Good looking." I said and hung up the phone.

I went back to sleep immediately after only to be woken up when I felt somebody getting in the bed with me. Being a street nigga for majority of ya life made you a light sleeper. I didn't have to open my eyes to know that Yanni had gotten in the bed with me. I smelled the mango butter oil as soon as she opened the door. She positioned herself right up under me and just like that, from the feel of her skin against mine, I was sleep again.

Waking up with Yanni in my arms had a nigga dick on brick. I was trying hard to be respectful, but I wanted to bend that ass over, pregnant or not. I wanted the pussy. Her hair was all over her head and her mouth was open, but she still looked sexy as fuck. I kissed the side of her neck and got up to shower and start the day. I had to get up with Haz and

Twist, so they knew to look out for that pussy nigga Black. When I got out of the shower Yanni was sitting on the edge of the bed.

"It's two in the afternoon. Why you let me sleep so long?" She asked.

She turned around and saw me standing in front of her dick swinging looking like a king and she couldn't take her eyes off me.

"Well damn." She said biting her bottom lip. She came over to me and surprised me when she wrapped both of her hands around my dick. I had never seen Yanni so bold. My dick bricked up at the feel of her hands. I grabbed her by her hair pulling her head back so I could kiss her neck, then her lips. I was never the type to be kissing bitches in the mouth and eating pussy and shit but Yanni had my ass open. I pulled the t-shirt she was wearing over her head and she was naked underneath. The swollen belly took nothing away from her sexy ass at all. I wanted her but I didn't want her to regret it later. I laid her back on the bed and kissed her from her lips until I was face to face with her wet pussy. She smelled like mango butter, but her pussy smelled like vanilla. I didn't think twice before I kissed it and took her clit in my mouth sucking it hard and then licking it softly; she grabbed a hand full of my dreads and pulled them a little.

"Fuck Qua!" She yelled out.

I stuck my tongue as far in her pussy as it would go licking upward so I touched her g-spot every time. She squeezed my tongue with her pussy muscles and literally flooded my mouth with her juices. I continued to eat her pussy until she started trying to close her legs with my head still between them.

"Ok Qua. I can't take it!"

I stood up leaning over her, so I wasn't on her stomach. She grabbed my face and licked my lips before kissing me.

She opened her legs wide and grabbed my dick putting it at the entrance of her pussy. I grabbed her hands before she was able to slide my 11 inches inside of her.

"Chill Kiyan."

"No, I want it, I want it bad." She moaned making my dick jump.

"You're pregnant." I said trying to convince myself that we shouldn't be doing this.

"So, you don't wanna fuck me cuz I'm fat." She said with her lip poked out.

"Nice try." I told her knowing that her ass was trying to use reverse psychology on a nigga. She started moving her hips upward, so the very tip of my dick was coated in her juices.

"Umm Fuck me Qua. I wanna feel you so bad baby." She moaned against my lips before kissing me again. Her sexy ass had won the battle. I was trying hard to fight it but her moans and her laying under me looking sexy as fuck had a nigga weak. Her fuck faces was everything, her pussy was tight and wet. I couldn't fight her ass any longer as I slowly slid inside of her inch by inch. Her pussy was gripping the shit out of my dick and I felt weak in the fuckin knees as soon as I was all in. I had never had pussy this good and now that I was in it, I hope her ass knew that it was mine and I was willing to kill behind it and die behind it, no cap. I stood up so I didn't hurt her stomach. I held her legs open wide and watched as my dick went in and out of her. I massaged her clit while I fucked her hard and had her cumming again and again.

"Turn that ass around." I told her.

She did what she was told and turned around tooting her ass in the air and arching her back as much as she could. I opened to her ass cheeks and licked between them. Her young ass had me doing some wild shit.

"Ohhh yes baby." She moaned out. I licked her ass and ate her pussy from the back until she came yet again and then I slid deep inside of her. Shit felt so good, I gripped her waist and fucked the shit out of her until I came deep inside of her. I laid beside her and she crawled up under me breathing hard.

"The fuck you breathing hard for. I did all the work."

She laughed. "Shut up."

"I tried to be respectful. You got me in here poking my baby girl in the head and shit. "

"Her ass will be just fine."

It got quiet, both of us with a lot of shit on our minds.

"I feel guilty that I'm so happy with you. It hasn't even been a year yet and yes I'm grieving still but you make it better and I don't know if I'm supposed to have better so soon after he left me."

I looked into her eyes and saw confusion, pain, guilt. Things I was familiar with and all I wanted to do was take that all away from her. I never believed in soul mates or no shit like that, but this had to be that.

"I lost my brother when I was ten and after that, every birthday I had or even if I had a good day, I felt guilty cause he wasn't able to do the same things but eventually I realized that my brother lives through me. My life isn't just mine; it's ours and he would want me to live it to the fullest."

"Did the pain ever go away?" She asked sadly.

"Nah, you just learn to live with it, but shit does get better."

"I'm sorry to ruin our moment talking about him."

"I wanna know what you feeling and what you thinking. Don't ever feel like you gotta hide shit from me. Always keep it a hunnit and I swear I'll do whatever I got to do to make sure you straight. I wanna keep you happy and that's saying a lot because I ain't ever gave a fuck about nobody else's happiness." Of course, her cry baby ass started crying. "You making me feel like a pussy right now with all that crying." I said.

"I just didn't think I could get true love twice in one lifetime." She said to me before sitting up in the bed. "Can we go see my Daddy?" She asked heading towards the bathroom.

"I gotta go bust a few moves. When I come back I'll take you to see ya pops. I don't want you going over there by yaself. I don't need y'all arguing and all that dumb shit stressing my baby girl."

"Why have I never seen this side of you before."

"It didn't exist."

$$

When I pulled up on the block, I noticed Twist standing in front of the trap. I got out and joined him. O always bitched about us not having to play the block. He was forever preaching that we didn't ever have to see the hood if we didn't want to, but it was something about that block work shit that I loved. The streets ain't never loved a soul but that didn't stop us from fuckin with her heavy. Now that I had Yanni I was starting to understand what he was saying.

"What's shaken?" I peaced Twist and stood next to him against his car.

"Ain't shit. I had to pick up that money from that nigga Nice, and D-Cash doubled his usual order, so I had to take care of that but that's about it until we gotta meet up with Jay and them later."

"Where Haz at?" I asked.

"I don't even know. I ain't speak to his bitch ass all day."

Before I could even reach for my phone to call this nigga shots rang out. I snatched my piece from my waist and bust back at the all black Impala with tinted windows. After they were gone, I turned to make sure Twist was good and he was.

"You good?" I asked.

"Yeah. Where you hit at?" He asked rushing over to me.

"Huh?" I asked suddenly feeling dizzy as everything went black.

Chapter Eighteen
QUINN ISSACS

Niko was in Miami for the next week and some change and a bitch was so happy. So happy that I had finally agreed to let Haz take me out for some food and drinks. We had been talking and texting all the time and finally I had some free time and no black eyes. As soon as we sat at the table Haz's phone started blowing the fuck up.

"You and Meesha back together or something?" I asked him suspiciously.

"Naw but let me get this; that hoe Sienna been blowing me up." He said answering his phone.

"Yo." He got quiet but I didn't miss the fear in his eyes. He jumped up from the table and so did I. "We gotta go." He damn near ran to the car with me struggling to keep up in the four and a half inch heels I was rocking. When we got to the car, I finally asked him what the fuck was going on.

"Qua got shot; we gotta get to the hospital."

"What. Oh My God. Is he ok?"

"I don't know yet." I pulled out my phone and called Yanni. I didn't want to upset her, but she was just telling me earlier how she was falling in love with Qua and she needed to be there.

"Yanni, I need you to meet me at the hospital please."

"Quinn, did that nigga put his hands on you again?" She asked.

"Just please come Kiyan."

"I'm on my way."

We made it to the hospital and Twist was in the waiting area. There was blood all over his hands and shirt. His tall frame was leaned over with his head in his hands like he was praying. Before we could even make it over to where Twist was sitting Yanni came into the hospital and walked over to me. She looked at me and noticed that I was fine, then over to Haz and inside the waiting room at Twist. I tried to grab her, but her pregnant ass flew over to Twist and grabbed his arm causing him to look up at her.

"Where is he?"

"Calm down Yanni. He's in the back but he gone be good."

"What happened?" She asked with a faraway look in her eyes.

"He got shot on th....."

"Shot? No, no, no this can't be happening to me again. I need to see him now." She started crying.

I grabbed her and pulled her into a hug as she started to panic. I didn't think this shit through when I called her. She had been here before and I couldn't imagine how she was feeling right now.

"Calm down Yanni. I'm sure he's fine but you need to calm down for the baby."

"Oh God, Quinn, I can't breathe. I can't do this shit again; I can't do it! I swear I can't take it. Oh God, I can't breathe." She started to hyperventilate; I was panicking right along with her ass. I had no idea what to do. Out of nowhere, Qua came rushing towards us. When he noticed us all surrounding Yanni while she tried to stop crying and catch her breath, he damn near knocked us all over to get to her. His shoulder was bandaged up in two places.

"Baby, what's the matter?" He dropped the papers in his hand and grabbed both sides of her face. When she saw him, I could see the relief in her tear-filled eyes. She stood to her feet and wrapped her arms around his neck. I could tell that he was in pain bending down to hug her, but he ignored it; his only concern was her.

"They said you got shot. I thought you were..." She couldn't even say the words and that brought tears to my eyes.

Rome's death had her so fragile and I felt like shit for calling her. He tried to peel her arms from around his neck, but she wasn't having it.

"Baby, look at me." She let him go and looked him over.

"I'm good. You know I ain't leaving ya spoiled ass no time soon. You gotta calm down for my baby girl." He wiped her face with his shirt and kissed her lips. She was calming down but still held him tightly by the waist. She looked like a child with his 6'2 frame towering over her 5'5 frame.

"Who called her?" He asked.

"Guilty. I'm sorry but when Haz got the call we didn't know what the fuck was going on." I said.

"Sienna called me screaming and shit like they took you out or some shit." Haz said.

"I ain't call you cuz they told me when I got here that he was good. Bullets went in and out both in the shoulder. He just lost a lot of blood, so he passed out." Twist said. Him and Haz pulled Qua in a brotherly hug and it was so cute. As long as I had known them, they were thick as thieves and I admired the loyalty.

"Aight, the fuck. Y'all acting like a bunch of bitches." Qua said laughing.

"Love y'all for real. I ain't tryna have shit happen to my brothers." Twist said.

"We love you too bitch." Haz and Qua said at the same time causing us all to laugh. We went our separate ways with Haz eventually dropping me off at home so he could get up with Qua and Twist about what happened. When we pulled up in front of the house I shared with Niko depression greeted me at the door.

"You don't gotta stay with that bitch ass nigga."

"What you mean?" I asked.

"I mean I saw the sadness in ya eyes as soon as we pulled up."

"You wouldn't understand."

"Try me." He said.

"It's complicated."

"Ain't nothing complicated about letting that nigga beat ya ass. Can't nobody force you to get out. You gotta want that for yaself."

I fought back the tears because I honestly had no idea if I would ever be free of Niko.

"Thanks for everything Hassan."

He leaned over and kissed me on the lips making me blush.

"You got it." He said. He waited for me to open the door before he pulled off. It was a little after midnight and all I wanted to do was have a shower and go to bed.

When I walked into the living room and turned on the light, I pissed on myself. Niko was standing by the window. He had a gun hanging down by his side and a bottle of Hennessey in his other hand. I was literally frozen in place. I was scared. I knew that he saw me getting out of Haz's car and possibly saw the kiss. He wasn't supposed to be back until next week, which is the only reason I agreed to let Haz drop me off. I wouldn't have been out this late if Qua hadn't of gotten hurt. His eyes were blood shot red and he looked soulless. I had seen him mean and evil, but I had never seen the hatred that I was seeing in his eyes now.

"Niko."

Before I could say anything else, he threw the bottle of Hennessey at my head. I ducked just in time for the bottle to hit the wall behind me and shatter. I tried to run but I fell flat on my face in these dumb ass heels. Even though I fell, I still tried to get the fuck out of there. I crawled towards the front door, but Niko grabbed me by my hair and dragged me back towards the kitchen.

"You got a nigga bringing ya hoe ass to my fuckin house! Bitch you must wanna die tonight!" He roared as he slammed the gun into the back of my head. Out of instinct, my hands went up to my head, and I felt blood. Niko hit me in the head with the gun again and I swear this time the nigga used every bit of strength he had. I fell flat on my stomach. He kicked me in my side twice before I finally rolled over on my back. I screamed out in agony. My body felt like it was on fire; every single thing hurt. I was dizzy and I fought hard to stay conscious, but it was so hard.

"Niko please." I managed to get out.

"Please what hoe?" He slurred as he took his dick out and peed on me. I had never felt so low in my life. I could hear him laughing as I continued to slip in and out of darkness.

"If I can't have you nobody else can." I heard Niko growl.

I opened my eyes just in time to see him plunge the knife into my stomach. I said a prayer asking for forgiveness and praying that God would bring Yanni through this without her breaking completely down. The last thing I saw before I slipped into the light was Niko smiling at me as he stabbed me once again.

Chapter Nineteen
DOMINICK NIKO MENA

Damn, I panicked after stabbing Quinn twice; it was blood everywhere. I didn't mean to do the shit. I just snapped. I hated a sneaky ass bitch and she was forever doing some bullshit. I washed the blood off my hands and the knife putting it in the dishwasher and turned it on. I know y'all thinking why would I put my hands on her and all that other shit but in my experience the only way to rule a woman was with a fist.

I grew up in a house where my older sister molested me and when I told my mother she told me to stop actin like a punk. I was nine at the time and she forced me to eat her pussy and fuck her until I was 14 and strong enough to beat that hoe's ass. I would fuck her every time I saw her and my mother too. Til this day them hoes knew not to ever cross my path because I would kill them both. I loved Quinn; she was the first woman I had loved since my mother and sister so for some reason I hated her too. I wanted to make her happy but then again, I couldn't stand to see her happy. The shit was crazy even I couldn't comprehend it.

"Quinn, Quinn can you hear me?" I shook her but she didn't move.

It seemed like the puddle of blood was growing bigger by the second, so I knew she was dead. I hurried to the security room and deleted everything that was on the surveillance, then I turned it off so it wouldn't record me leaving. I was still supposed to be in Miami, so no one knew I was here. I turned my phone off and put it in my pocket so I could destroy it later. I changed clothes and left as quietly as I came.

She was dead and I hated to just leave her there like that but she left me with no choice. She should have known better than to ever bring a nigga to my fuckin house. Quinn had no one to blame for this shit but herself.

My next show after Miami was in Baltimore so I headed that way. When the police came looking for me, I would just say that I came to Baltimore earlier than expected. Money was power and I was sure I could pay some hotel clerk to make the receipt say whatever the fuck I wanted it to say. As for that nigga Haz I hope he didn't think he was going to disrespect my house and get away with that shit. I was going to kill that nigga and his bitch ass friends. It was time that these niggas stopped playing with me. They thought that because a nigga could sing that I was pussy, but I was far from that and he was going to be dealt with for this shit.

Chapter Twenty
QUASIEM 'QUA' SHAKUR

I can't believe that bitch ass nigga Black really shot me. I had nobody to blame but me because I didn't think he was going to come at me so soon if at all. But that nigga was living on borrowed time. If my shorty wasn't so upset behind this shit, I would have been putting a bullet in that nigga face tonight.

My arm was hurting like a motha fucka. I'm just happy it was my left arm cuz I'm a right-handed nigga and woulda been assed out. When we got home, I ran Yanni a bath to calm her nerves. I didn't want her to stress the baby or no shit like that, so I needed her all the way calm.

I found her in the guest room with her head in her hands crying.

"Lil Mama, what's wrong?" I grabbed her pulling her up off the bed and onto my lap.

"I just don't want that one horrible incident to control my whole life. I automatically thought the worst; I couldn't even control myself." She said.

"Not only did the nigga get shot and killed, he was shot and killed in front of you. He died in your arms, you carrying his child and it's still new. It hasn't even been a year yet. You gotta give yourself time to heal Kiyan." I kissed her neck and then her lips.

"I love you so much already and I can't lose you. I know that all this is new to you and that you're use to looking out for just you but please when you out there in them streets I need you to think about me and her. I need you to just be aware that if anything happens to you, I'll die Quasiem." I ain't never had nobody love me like that and a nigga was honored that she chose me.

"You the Queen Yanni. I'm following ya lead baby. You gotta nigga so open that ain't no bullets keeping me away from you. I love you and I ain't ever said that to no other woman, not even my mother. I'll always put you first. I'll always think about you. I'll always come back to you."

"Promise?"

"I promise."

I took her clothes off her and carried her into the bathroom sitting her inside of the bath.

"I thought you was about to give me some dick." She said rolling her eyes. I laughed.

"You can sit on this dick later. Haz and Twist in the basement waiting for me."

When I got down to my fully furnished basement, Twist was in the refrigerator as Haz was sitting down with a drink in his hand playing Call of Duty.

"Bout time nigga." Twist said.

"Had to make sure Shorty straight."

"Aight, so who dying?" Haz said. He was always the chill one, but that nigga had more bodies under his belt than me and Twist.

"That nigga Black."

"Mace brother. I thought that nigga was locked up for stealing pussy." Twist said.

"I don't know how much time you get for a rape charge but that nigga home. Sienna called me early this morning. Said that nigga was up at the strip club talking big shit about how he was gone body me. The whole reason I went on the block was to holla at y'all about the nigga."

"Say less; that nigga will be gone soon enough." Haz said.

"Aye you straight?" Twist asked.

"Ain't no thing to a G. Shit gone get on my nerves more than anything."

"So, you in love kid?" Haz asked smiling all goofy and shit.

"Yeah, it's looking like that."

"Damn, this shit crazy. I never thought I would see the day my boy settle down." Twist said.

"I know; shit crazy but what the fuck was you doing with Niko bitch?"

"That's bout to be my bitch as soon as she stop fuckin with that pussy. I already wanna put a bullet in his head." Haz said.

"Meesha ain't having that." I said laughing. That bitch had been going crazy since he cut her off.

"Fuck Meesha." Haz replied.

"Damn, you tryna kill the nigga over his girl?" Twist said.

"The nigga can't keep his hands to himself. You know I hate a nigga that wanna beat his bitch but won't even step to a nigga." Haz said looking frustrated.

Haz's mother was killed by her husband when he was 13. His step-pops then turned the gun on himself like the pussy he was because he feared going the jail. It was a soft spot for him so I could only imagine him fucking with a bitch in that same situation was hard for him. We kicked it for a few hours, drinking and smoking, until Yanni called me to come get in the bed with her. After them niggas got done clowning me, they left. Neither of them niggas lived too far away from me, so I wasn't worried about them getting home safely.

Chapter Twenty-One
HASSAN 'HAZ' SHAHID

The whole time I was at Qua's house I couldn't get Quinn out of my head. It was now three am and she wasn't answering the phone, so I was on my way back to her house. I didn't give a fuck if that nigga was there or not. When I pulled up in front of the house, I felt funny as shit. When I approached the house, the door was slightly open so that made me pull my gun before I went inside. I walked into the house and immediately noticed the smell of blood in the air, but I didn't see anybody. I walked further into the house and that's when I saw her laid out in the kitchen in a puddle of blood. I was a nigga who had killed more times than I could count but I had never seen so much blood. I couldn't even tell where the shit was coming from. Just seeing her like this took me back to being 13 years old and finding my mother's dead body after her punk ass husband took her away from her only son.

I finally snapped out of my daze and walked over to her. I had no choice but to step in the blood because it was just so much. I grabbed her wrist and was shocked that she still had a faint pulse. I looked around. I saw her house phone sitting on the kitchen table. I grabbed it and called 911. The ambulance and police came in less than five minutes. They tried to get her alert, but she was still out cold. Them pigs thought they was going to question me, but I wasn't about to play with them mothafuckas. They could do their own fuckin job. As soon as the ambulance pulled off, I was right behind them. I was headed to the hospital. When I made it to the hospital, they were rushing her to the back. I approached the receptionist desk.

"The one they just rushed back there, Quinn Issacs. Can you please get me an update as soon as possible." I said.

"No problem sir. Please have a seat in the private waiting room." She said to me noticing the blood all over me. I entered the waiting room and didn't want to call Qua. I had witnessed the way Yanni reacted earlier and I didn't want to put her or the baby in another stressful situation, but this was serious. I didn't know how to reach Quinn's family or no shit like that, so I had to call him. He answered the phone half sleep. It was about 5 am by now.

"You straight?" He answered.

"I found Quinn in her house damn near dead. She had a lil pulse when I got there. They rushed her to the hospital and I'm here now but they ain't give me no updates or nothing."

"Damn. Aight we'll be up there. Hold ya head."

The shit was so crazy to me. When I found out that nigga Niko was beating her ass, I wanted to be done with her. I know from experience that most abuse victims don't leave willingly. I didn't want to ever be caught up in this situation again. I had lived it and it had ended the way they always end... in death. Quinn was fighting for her life and I would bet my last dollar that Niko was behind this shit.

Twist walked into the waiting room and took a seat next to me.

"You good?" He asked.

"Yeah I'm straight."

Twist and Qua was the only family I had. I was 23 years old, Qua 23 and Twist 24. We had a code of loyalty that a lot of these niggas would never understand. I would happily lay down and die for them niggas and I knew they would do the same for me. I appreciated that they always came running when a nigga needed them.

"Qua called me. He was trying to calm Yanni ass down before they get here. You aight?" He asked me again because even though I said I was good I wasn't quite good, and he could sense the shit.

"When I found my moms, she was just like that. Laying in the kitchen in a puddle of blood at the hands of some punk ass nigga."

"It's gone be aight."

Qua and Yanni came in a few minutes later. She was red in the face and her eyes were puffy like she had been crying but she was calmer than she was before.

"You good?" Qua asked me and I told him the same thing

I told Twist a few minutes ago that I was straight. Finally, the doctor came out to let us know what the fuck was going on.

"Family of Quinn Issacs?"

"Yes, that's us." Yanni said.

"Ms. Issacs lost a lot of blood, but she is alive in critical condition. She was stabbed twice in the abdomen we were able to perform surgery and there was no major damage from the stab wounds, but she also suffered blunt force trauma to the back of her head. She was struck a few times with a hard object. Luckily there was no fracturing to the skull. We have her in a medically induced coma because there is some swelling on the brain. With brain injuries it's typically a 50/50 chance of survival. We will monitor her closely and when the swelling on the brain goes down, if it goes down, we will wake her up to determine if there has been any long term damage. She's strong and lucky to be alive."

"Can I see her?" Yanni asked.

"Yes, two at a time." She said.

"Go ahead Haz. I need a minute." Yanni said before walking out of the waiting room followed by Qua.

When I got to the room, it was cold and quiet. Her head was bandaged and she had a tube coming out of her mouth. The beeping noises from the machines didn't do anything to put a nigga at ease. Despite all the bruising and swelling she still looked beautiful as if she was just sleeping. I walked over to her, grabbed her hand and kissed it.

"You know you got a shooter behind you baby girl and I'mma make sure that nigga pay for every black eye, busted lip, and bruise he ever put on you. I swear I'mma see him about this shit. I know if you made it out of that house alive that you will make it outta this bed alive. I'm waiting on you so don't take too long." I told her and kissed her hand again.

I walked out of the room feeling like this situation was

going to harden me even more. I wanted blood and I wanted it now. When I got home, I searched that nigga Niko's schedule and saw that he cancelled his show in Connecticut. I would keep a close watch on his bitch ass knowing that his social media would lead me right to him.

Chapter Twenty-Two
KIYAN 'YANNI' MAJORS

Walking into that room was the hardest thing I had ever done. The police were talking about it was an open case, but I knew exactly who had done this. I tried to tell her repeatedly to leave that nigga alone, but she was convinced that she loved him. She got defensive anytime you bashed him or talked about him so eventually I had to fall back and let her live her own life. When her mother moved, I offered to get her an apartment; even asked Qua if she could stay in the guest room, but she declined. Now I'm feeling like I should have made her come. I knew that nobody was to blame for this but Niko but that didn't stop me from wondering why it had to come to this. Qua was right by my side as I entered the room and walked over to the bed. I kissed her cheek and held her hand thinking about what a fucked up two days this had been.

"Best Friend, I need you to be ok. You've never missed a moment in my life and I damn sure can't have you missing the birth my first child. You mean the world to me, Quinn, and I'm feeling fucked up that I didn't try harder to get you to leave that nigga. I should have been there for you like you're always there for me, and I'm so sorry. Just please wake up."

I was literally tired of tears at that point. Like, enough is enough. I felt a sharp pain in the bottom of my back.

"Ouch." I said because the shit literally caught me off guard.

"You ok?" Qua asked concerned as always.

"Yeah, it's my back."

"You been stressing the fuck outta my baby these past couple of days. You need to lay down or some shit." He fussed.

I loved how he loved my daughter and I knew that if he had breath in his body, she would have a father in her life.

"I'm fine. I just..." Before I could finish my sentence, I felt a gush of liquid pour out of my vagina.

"Fuck!" I yelled.

"What?"

"My water broke."

"Come on; we gotta get you upstairs."

"I can't just leave her by herself." I said feeling bad.

"We called her moms hours ago. She should be here soon and I'll check on her every hour." He said while dragging my ass out of the room.

My back had been hurting since I got the call that Qua was shot the day before, but I didn't think anything of it. When we got to labor and delivery, they wasted no time getting me settled in a room and called my doctor. I was nervous as fuck. I was only eight and a half months and I was scared that something would be wrong with her but at the same time I couldn't wait to see her. When they finally checked me, I was seven centimeters. Apparently, the back pain was contractions and my dumb ass had been in active labor since yesterday.

Two Hours Later...

"I see her head baby." Qua said excitedly. "Just one more push baby. You got this; she almost here."

"I'm tired." I said with tears in my eyes. I had been pushing for over an hour and this stubborn little girl had yet to make an entrance. Qua grabbed my hand and kissed my lips.

"You can do this shit. One more push Lil Shorty." And with one more push my baby girl entered the world screaming at the top of her lungs. They placed her on my chest and started to wipe her off with a blanket and clear her nose and mouth. I looked at her and smiled. God heard me when I asked him to give Rome back to me and he did. Even before her features were developed, she looked exactly like him and I couldn't do anything but cry tears of joy. I had lost this great love, but I got it back times two in Italy and Qua. I was the luckiest woman in the world.

When they got us all cleaned up and in a recovery room I sat back watching Qua hold Italy in his arms. He was so in love he kept kissing her little forehead and she was looking up at him; it was so precious. Finally, the princess was sleep and Qua put her in her bassinet and came over to me.

"She's so beautiful." He said.

"She looks just like him." I commented. "I know that you were there during the whole pregnancy but now that she's here, I just wanna make sure that this is what you want. You've never even had a real relationship and now you've got a girl and a kid." I said.

"You know I'm not the type of nigga to be forced into anything. I'm here because I want to be here." Qua kissed my lips and no sooner than he pulled away from me my Daddy was walking in the room.

"What are you doing here?" I asked him on the verge of tears. I had a lot of shit go down within 48 hours and I was overly emotional and annoyed.

"Can I talk to my daughter alone?" He said to Qua but never took his eyes off me.

"You cool with that?" Qua asked me and I shook my head yes. Giving him the green light to leave us in the room alone.

He walked towards the bassinet looking at Italy briefly before he came back towards the bed.

"The offer to do the right thing and give the baby to your Aunt Janine to raise still stands." He said.

"If that's why you're here you can get the fuck out. I'm not giving my baby up for adoption and I'm not discussing this again."

"I did everything I could possibly think of to give you and your sister a better life but neither of you appreciate that shit. I never wanted you to be caught up with a low life drug dealer like Rome. I protected you from him but now you want to be burdened with his child at only 19. Why would you do this?" He asked trying to sound sincere.

"What the fuck do you mean you protected me from Rome?" Fuck all that other shit he was talking; that statement didn't sit well with me.

"I tried to protect you from him." For the first time in my life I didn't see my Daddy who I loved so much. I saw a cold-blooded evil bastard.

Tears fell from my eyes and my heart was beating out of my chest. Was he saying what I thought he was saying? I couldn't stomach it if my father had done something to Rome.

"Did you kill him?" I asked needing to know.

"I'm a businessman baby girl, you know that." He said with a smug look on his face.

Not a direct yes or a direct no. The cry that escaped my mouth alerted my baby girl. She started to cry and before I knew it Qua had entered the room, gun dangling casually by his side with fire in his eyes.

"We got a fuckin problem?" Qua asked calmly.

"This between me and my daughter nigga." My Daddy grimaced.

"Ya daughter. Nigga this my bitch. She calls me Daddy now." Qua said standing directly in front of me.

"This what you want, Kiyan? A baby and some thug ass nigga that's going to make you a widow or a prison wife." My daddy yelled at me.

"Daddy, just leave." I said, tears still running down my face.

I stared in the face of the man that I had been head over heels in love with my entire life. I was always a Daddy's girl and I felt that he loved me unconditionally but as memories ran through my mind, I realized that my Daddy's love had always been conditional. He loved me if I was doing what he wanted me to do, as long as I was living the life that he wanted me to live. Kaycie had always been right about him. There was no room for fuck ups or imperfections, and I was seeing that now.

"I love you Daddy." I said to his back as he walked out of the door and out of my life.

I had a feeling that those words would be the last that I would speak to my Daddy, and I wanted them to be positive. He didn't even respond which made me cry harder. Qua wrapped his arms around me and kissed my forehead. I pulled back from him and punched him in the chest.

"Ya bitch? Really nigga?" I said causing him to laugh.

Chapter Twenty-Three
AKACIA 'KAYCIE' MAJORS

Somebody had been calling me from a blocked number for a few days now and I had been ignoring it thinking it was Uncle Kevon but finally I decided to answer.

"Who the fuck is this?" I asked nastily.

"It's me Niko. I'm hiding out and I need you to get here with me."

"Nigga everybody looking for ya ass. Why the fuck would you try to kill Quinn like that? I don't like that hoe but she ain't deserve all that." I said.

"I don't give a fuck about that shit. I need you here with me Kay."

"Ok baby. Text me ya location. I'll be there as soon as I can." I said not having any intentions on going to be with his ass.

When I wanted him, he ain't want me. Now the nigga wanted for attempted murder and he wanna be all on me. I walked into my house and saw a bloody Uncle Kevon in the living room on the floor while my father stomped him. I rushed over to break it up, jumping between him and Daddy giving Uncle Kevon time to stand to his feet.

"Stop Daddy. You going to kill the nigga." I yelled.

He had been so outta character lately I was starting to wonder if the nigga was on that shit.

"You coming at me and I get it but while you so worried about Kaycie, did you tell her you murdered her mother and her real father." Kevon yelled.

Immediately, I snatched my hands off my father's chest where I was trying to hold him back from Kevon. I stared up at him feeling like the tough wall I had built up all these years had crumbled in an instant. Tears pooled my eyes and I felt sick to my stomach.

"Daddy, did you?" I asked in a childlike voice.

"She was a junkie Kaycie. She let that nigga come back into her life and get her hooked back on that shit. I wasn't raising kids with a junkie, so I killed her. The drugs would have eventually killed her anyway. It's no big deal."

"You killed my parents and then raised me like the shit never happened? Daddy, how could you?" I cried from my gut because I was already fucked up, but this shit was really going to fuck my head up.

How could you murder two people and look their child in the eyes every day and not feel even an ounce of guilt.

"It's a lot of shit you and your sister don't know about. I did some fucked up shit, but your father is a monster." Kevon said just before the bullet from my father's gun entered his skull.

I screamed, horrified as I watched his body hit the floor with a loud thud. My heart was racing, my hands were sweaty, and I could not believe this shit just happened.

"Baby girl. You know I love you and your sister. I just want my girls to have the best life possible. Your mother couldn't help me give y'all the best. She was fucking up our perfect family and I couldn't have that." I was in shock. I just stood there listening and crying.

His phone rang and he picked it up. I could hear his assistant since they were on Facetime.

"Qua just came here with a gun and took everything he's ever recorded. He had some guy with him that was a damn computer whiz hacker or whatever. He said he's not fuckin with you on any level anymore." She said.

My father or should I say Omere, calmly talked to her like he didn't just kill a man and confess to murdering my parents.

"I'll handle Qua. Send clean-up to my house as soon as possible." He added before hanging up.

He walked over to me and kissed me on the cheek. It felt like the kiss of death to me. After he left the room, I stood there for almost a half hour getting myself together before I went up to my room to pack a bag. Niko had sent me a Baltimore address and being that my father had just dropped a bomb on me, hiding out with Niko no longer sounded so bad. I packed a bag and by the time I came back downstairs Kev's body was gone. I looked around the house knowing I wouldn't be back anytime soon. I had always needed my mother. I had always felt left out because of Daddy's relationship with Yanni and on top of that the many women he had in and out of this damn house had no interest in mothering two girls. They were just here for the money and dick. My Daddy was famous, on TV, on the radio, loved all over the world and yet he was nothing like he appeared to be on the outside.

Chapter Twenty-Four
HASSAN 'HAZ' SHAHID

"I been looking everywhere for this nigga; that bitch done got ghost." I told Qua after we left the studio from erasing all his shit off the hard drive at O's studio.

"He gotta pop out sooner or later." He told me.

"On my Mama I'm sending that nigga to his maker as soon as he does."

"So, you feeling shorty like that? You bout to dead a nigga over her."

"Nothing you ain't already done for yours."

"Respect." Qua said.

"I'm feeling her heavy and since that night I been thinking bout my moms and that shit got a nigga out for blood for real."

"That pussy in the public eye; he can't hide forever."

"Facts. But how's Daddy day care treating you?"

"Shit crazy. I went from doing me, hugging the block, chasing a bag, murdering any nigga that even looked at me wrong to having a girl and a baby. At first, I thought I wouldn't love her unconditionally because she's not biologically mine but just being a part of this and watching her grow, the fact that's she's not really mine means nothing at all bra. That little girl is my heart and I've already made up my mind that regardless of what happens with me and Yanni, I got Italy forever." He said.

"I ain't never heard you talk like this. I'm proud of you kid." I honestly told him.

Me, him and Twist were a bunch of broken little boys that got dealt some fucked up hands but to see the way we turned all that shit around and we was still standing ten toes down, winning wars, making money and being strong, loyal, powerful black men. That shit made a nigga proud.

"I'm thinking about getting this music shit popping for real. I never thought I would want outta the streets but with people depending on me I gotta move different." He said.

"As you should. Ain't none of these rap niggas out here fuckin with you blood. You got real talent."

"I want you and Twist with me though. You a singing ass nigga and Twist got Bars for days. I can't see myself leaving my brothers in the trenches. Truth is if y'all in I'm in. Blood in Blood out, if I walk, we all gotta walk." He said and I understood him 100 percent.

"I'll think about it."

$$

When I walked into Quinn's hospital room Yanni was coming out.

"Damn sis. You don't look like you had a baby three weeks ago." I said gassing her up.

"What can I say? My snapback game strong as fuck." She laughed and exited the room.

"How you feeling today?" I asked Quinn kissing her on her forehead.

"Ugly." She said pouting.

"Cut the dumb shit out. You look beautiful." Quinn was light skin so even though the swelling had gone down a lot she still had some deep bruising on her face.

"The healing process is just so slow. I'm ready to get the fuck out of here." She complained.

"You had swelling on the brain; those people were talking about you wasn't going to make it. Fuck them bruises. You better thank the big homie upstairs that you even here right now." I told her truthfully.

"I know. I don't mean to complain. I'm just drained, ready to start over. I wanna thank you for saving my life. If it wasn't for you coming back, I would be dead." She replied.

"It's all good. No need to thank me."

"So modest. This Haz that I've been getting to know is nothing like what I hear in the streets."

"I gotta be a goon in the streets, that's how I survive.

Mother fuckas ain't never going to get to see what you see and that's on my mama." She smiled.

I loved to see shorty smile. I was getting caught up with Quinn and that's some shit I never intended to do so soon after Meesha. I wanted to chill and be single but shit never goes how you plan, and I was starting to see that now. It had been five months since I broke up with Meesha and word on the street was that she had been evicted and was living place to place. I ain't going to lie and say the shit didn't bother me but I was done with her and didn't want to get in the habit of taking care of her. She wouldn't understand that I was just helping her bum ass out. She would think I still wanted her. If I did that, I would never be rid of her and I wasn't the type of nigga to keep loose ends open. When I was done, I was done.

"I need to start looking for a place when I get out of here. I can't go back to that house."

"I already cleared that shit out and put all ya stuff in storage. I can set you up in an apartment before your released. Just let me know what you want and it's done.

"Just like that?" She asked.

"Just like that Ma. I keep telling you I got you."

Chapter Twenty-Five
KIYAN 'YANNI' MAJORS

"Oh, Baby I'm about to cum." I moaned against Qua's lip as he sat up on the couch while I rode his dick.

"Cum all over this dick then." He said before biting my bottom lip and then kissing me.

I couldn't get enough of Qua since my six weeks was up

last month. I couldn't stay off his dick if I tried. I was addicted and very much in love all over again. I hadn't seen my Daddy, or my sister and I was cool with that. Qua and Italy were my family now and that's all that mattered.

I came hard and Qua was right behind me emptying his seeds inside of me. I kissed his lips and then got up and headed to the bathroom to freshen up. When I came back out Qua was in the booth laying down a verse to a song we were doing together called "Trap Love". Qua had raw talent and the fact that he chose to seriously dive into the music business because he now had me and Italy to think about legit made me love him even more. I admired him and knew that I would always do any and everything to keep him happy. After he was done putting it down, he came out of the booth.

"It's ya turn Lil Mama." He said to me.

I was nervous but I was so ready to get over this fear and get back to me. Singing was a part of me that Johnny stole when he raped me, and I was taking it back. I hadn't stepped foot in the booth since I was raped and as I entered I felt anxious and scared but when I looked through the glass at Qua I knew that he would never let anybody hurt me and that was enough to have me singing my heart out. It felt so good and with every word I sung the anxiety faded away. I was home in the booth and me and my baby were creating magic together. When I finished, I came out of the booth and Qua played it back for me. I was so geeked. My voice sounded so perfect like I had never taken a break from singing in the first place.

"Damn baby, you made my dick hard." He said causing me to laugh.

"Shut up nasty."

Since Qua had taken everything he recorded from my Dad's studio he had a lot of his music and I was happy that he didn't lose any of his shit because knowing my Daddy he would have never given the music up as a way to punish Qua for fucking with me. Qua, Haz and Twist owned the studio we were in and that was another thing that had my Daddy pissed. A lot of artists were now coming to Qua's studio called 'The Trap House' and my daddy was losing business because of it.

When we finally got home, Quinn was sitting in her car in front of my door.

"Hey, how long you been here?" I asked.

"Not long. I saw you was on your way on 'Find Friends'," She said.

"Fuckin stalker. Wassup though?"

"Nothing, get in. I need to talk to you about something and I don't need Qua to hear us." She said making me nervous about what she could have to tell me.

"What's going on?"

"Look, when I tell you this please don't get mad at me." She said with watery eyes.

"Quinn you're scaring me and annoying me. Just tell me."

"I overheard Niko and your father talking one day about your Dad having Rome killed." She said with tears in her eyes.

I was suspicious after the comment my Daddy made at the hospital, but I was holding onto faith that he wouldn't do that to me.

"What? Why?" I asked.

"I don't know. All I heard was Niko tell him that the nigga he paid to do it wanted more money so he could get out of town."

"When was this?"

Quinn had just gotten out of the hospital a month ago after being there for like five weeks. So, I knew it couldn't be recent.

"Like six months ago." She replied crying.

"Six months ago!" I yelled. "Why the fuck are you just telling me this shit now?" I asked pissed the fuck off.

"I'm so sorry Yanni. When I heard that shit, I didn't know how to tell you; he's your father. Plus knowing how dangerous Niko was and how cold blooded your Dad was for doing that shit I was scared and I'm sorry." She said.

I knew that she was sorry but to keep something like that from me for so long seemed kind of unforgiveable. She was my best friend; my only fuckin friend and she should have come to me with the information whether she was scared or not. My mind was on overdrive thinking of all the times my father had consoled me and all the times he told me that it would be ok. The nights he sat beside my bed while I clutched a bloody dress until I fell asleep. He was laughing at me. He had caused the pain and had felt not one ounce of remorse. I was in a pain similar to the one that I felt when Rome died because in this moment, I knew that I would never have a father again.

I got out of the car not saying anything else to Quinn and got inside of my car. I had to confront my father about this shit, and I knew he would be nowhere but at the studio at this time, so I headed there. I entered his office to see him sitting at his desk with his young ass receptionist Cali in his lap. They were kissing and her halter top was pulled down exposing her titties.

"Omere, I need to talk to you." I said.

Cali hurried to pull her top up and looked embarrassed, but I gave not one fuck about that.

"Oh, I'm sorry. Hey Kiyan." She said.

I stayed quiet until she exited the room and closed the door behind her. My father looked me up and down before he smiled at me.

"You miss ya Daddy baby girl?" He asked me with a cocky look on his face.

"How could you do that to me Daddy? You knew I loved Rome and you had him killed?"

"Yeah Daddy, how could you do that? And while you explaining, you can tell us why you killed Mommy too? I left to get my mind right but I ain't forget about that shit." Kaycie said coming into the office and standing beside me.

I was shocked to see her. She had disappeared on everybody but what the fuck did she mean he killed our mother.

"Killed Mommy? What?" I asked.

"Since I have both of my beautiful daughters here I'll explain but only because I love my girls. As I told Akacia, your mother was a junkie. She started using when she was 17 right before she got pregnant with you Akacia. She was in love with your father and that punk ass nigga got her caught up on that shit." He said.

"Her father?" I interrupted.

"Yeah, I forgot to tell you he's not my real father. He's just been playing some cruel game taking care of the child that he made an orphan." Kaycie said with sad eyes.

"Anyway, he got her hooked on coke and eventually she graduated to crack and when I met her trying to buy drugs from one of my blocks, I was automatically infatuated with her. She had you with her Kaycie. You were about a week old and she was trying to trade you for drugs. I put the word out that no one was to sell to her ever again and I got her some help. For me it was love at first sight. Even though she was a fuckin junkie she was so beautiful. While she was going through rehab, I was the only one there for her. We fell in love and soon after she was pregnant with you Yanni. We were happy but she didn't love me like I loved her.

When you were a month old, Yanni, and Kiyan you a year, she saw your father Keith again and just like that she was back on drugs and in dope fiend love with the nigga. I got a call one night that she was at his apartment with him getting high and when I got there and saw her naked on a dirty mattress getting high with Keith, I blew both of their brains out. Keith's son Rome was about two at the time. I pointed my gun at that lil nigga and tried to kill his ass too, but the gun jammed. Before I could try again, I heard sirens and got the fuck out of there. Years later, the little nigga came to me for some work and since he didn't recognize me I let him work for me but the little bastard started fucking my daughter and not only that but he tried to go above my head and link with my connect. Bottom line is the nigga had to go. It wasn't all about you Kiyan. I hate Keith and everything attached to that nigga which includes that baby." He said.

"And what about me Daddy? Does that include me?" Kaycie said crying. It had been years since I seen her cry.

"You're the only exception baby girl. I loved you before I ever laid eyes on Keith, but it turns out that you're more like him that I ever wanted you to be."

My face was soaked in tears.

"You've been lying to us our whole lives. I don't care what the fuck she was doing or how much she hurt your feelings. She was our mother and you took that from us Daddy! And now my daughter will never get to know Rome. I'm just lucky that she'll have a father in Qua." I yelled.

"Fuck Qua. Who do you think pointed me in the direction of the niggas I hired to kill Rome. I told you to stay away from his ass. You shoulda listened." He laughed.

I didn't even have time to process his statement because out of nowhere Kaycie took a gun out of her purse and pointed it at Daddy. She had a crazy look in her eyes.

"Kaycie, put the gun down!" I told her.

"You've done too much Daddy. You've killed my mother, my father and the brother I never knew." She looked me in my eyes with tears falling from hers.

"I'm sorry Yanni. I'm sorry for treating you like shit. I was jealous but now I realize that none of this was your fault. I even told Johnny to go after you." She said breaking down.

"It's ok Kaycie. You were a little girl. You didn't know any better but just put the gun down. We can let Karma handle him. You don't have to throw ya life away on him Kaycie." I begged her. Not for my father but for her.

I could see so much pain in her eyes and I just wanted to get her some help so she could finally live.

"This is his Karma." She said and pulled the trigger.

POW!

The bullet went in his throat. I will never forget the look of shock on his face as he fell backwards onto the floor. I looked over at Kaycie and she too was shocked that she had actually done it. I ran over to my Daddy and kneeled down next to him, but he was already gone. eyes wide open. I broke down and cried not knowing what to do. He had done some evil things but that didn't change the fact that he was my father. The only parent I had ever known for the past 19 years and I didn't know what to do with all these emotions. I went over to my sister and hugged her tight. She had just killed our father and I'm sure she wasn't ok.

I hurried and grabbed a napkin from the box off my father desk before opening it up and taking his gun from the drawer. I rushed and put it in his hand with his finger on the trigger before pointing it in the direction we were just standing in and firing the gun. I didn't know if this would work but it was worth a try. At least this way Kaycie could say it was self-defense and I would back her up.

I could hear commotion in the hall. People running and screaming from the gun shots until finally security came into the office with guns pointed. Three hours later my father's body had been taken, our statements had been given and we were free to go. Upon walking out of the studio every news outlet and blog had microphones in our faces and taking pictures and shit of us walking out of the studio. They all wanted a statement and didn't give a fuck that our father had been killed. When I made it home, Qua was waiting for me but after what I had heard tonight about him and everything else, I just couldn't stand to look at him.

"What the fuck happened?"

"Some crazy shit but I need to get outta here. I can't stay here. I just came to get Italy." I told him trying to walk pass him, but he grabbed my arm pulling me back.

"You coming to get her for what? It's almost one in the morning. You ain't taking her nowhere." Looking in his face had tears flowing again. This had been one emotional ass year for me and I was over it.

"My father is dead, he killed my mother, he killed Kaycie's real father that I didn't know about, Rome was Kaycie's half-brother who my Daddy also had killed and he told me that you put him in contact with the niggas that he paid to kill Rome. Did you know?" I said.

"I didn't know shit about ya father killing no Rome until you told me what he said. He came to me and told me he needed some niggas to put in some work for him. I told him about some young hungry niggas that was out here wilding but he ain't ever mentioned no fuckin Rome to me. I don't even know if those the niggas he got to do the shit. Come on now. You know I wouldn't be laying up with you, playing Daddy to this nigga baby if I had some shit to do with that. I ain't no fuckin snake shorty. That ain't how I move." He said never breaking eye contact with me.

My head was all over the place and I really just needed time to figure all this shit out. I had been lied to my entire existence and right at that moment I didn't know who I could trust.

"I really need to be by myself to figure all this shit out." I said.

Qua looked pissed but grabbed his keys and walked out the door allowing me to do what I needed to do. I walked upstairs to the nursery and Italy was in her crib sleeping. She looked just like Rome. Not even a feature from me. She had his Hershey colored skin, his honey colored eyes, long curling eyelashes with the cutest button nose and perfect lips. She smiled in her sleep and I hoped that she could see her Daddy in her dreams. Rome was so genuine and treated me like glass. I loved him deeply and it hurt me to my core that he was dead because of some vendetta my father had for his. He was innocent in all of this and because my father got his heart broken by my mother 19 years ago, he was gone. I knew that I would have to let Rome go but that was difficult to do.

$$

On my way out of town I stopped to see Rome's mother Ms. Shannon. It was late but when she opened the door and saw me holding a baby that looked like her son she let me in. She hugged me tight and took Italy out of my arms. She held her up and stared at her before kissing her little checks. Tears slid down her face as she smiled at the precious baby girl her son had left behind. She sat down on the couch and I sat next to her. We sat in silence for a long time before I finally spoke.

"My father killed Rome." I said and broke down crying.

Ms. Shannon rubbed my back and I could hear the tears in her voice as well.

"Apparently, Rome's father and my mother had my sister together; he got her hooked on drugs, she left him just long enough to have me and then she went back. I'm so sorry Ms. Shannon; he killed Rome because of something that had nothing to do with either of us." I said.

I felt I owed her an explanation as to why she had to bury her 20-year-old son.

"Chiyan was your mother?" She asked.

"Yes, you knew her?" I asked, wanting to hear something about my mother from anyone but my father.

"Yes, we weren't friends. Just two young girls in love with the same man. I resented her and when she had your sister, I washed my hands of Keith. I couldn't believe that he could leave me and Rome like that and have a baby on me but when I saw your mother strung out on those drugs, I felt bad for her. I was happy that I got away from him because it could have been me. He took a perfectly beautiful girl and destroyed her. The night they were killed I dropped Rome off even though I didn't want to, but I had to get to work. I saw your mother and I begged her to leave Keith and get some help. She told me that she was already too far gone and couldn't be helped. She promised that she would take care of Rome for me. I hope she's taking care of my baby now." She said and got choked up.

"My father had me believing she died in child birth all these years. You can't imagine that guilt I felt thinking that I killed my own mother. My father is dead though."

"I know. I've been seeing it on the TV all night." She said.

"I'm really sorry Ms. Shannon about everything. I wish it could have been different. I just really need to get away from here for a while. I gotta clear my mind." I told her.

"You shouldn't run away from your problems Yanni." She told me.

"I have a man that loves me so much and I can't be what I need to be for him with all this pain and negative energy weighing me down. I have to go grieve and deal with it all. I gotta do this for me." I told her wiping the tears away.

"I don't blame you for any of this. Take care of yourself and bring my grandbaby by to see me from time to time." She said walking us to the door.

"I will." I promised.

$$

I drove to the beach house my father had in Virginia to hide out from the world. The house was passed down to him from his father before he died. When we were little, we would come here every summer because my father said within the short time he had known my mother this was the only place besides Jersey City that he had gotten to take her before she died. Of course, back then I didn't know that she was actually murdered, but it always made me feel good that she was actually within these walls once.

It had been three days since I left and all I did was cry and take care of Italy. Cali was all over the blogs claiming to be pregnant by my Daddy and saying how Kaycie should be in jail for what she did. That bitch didn't know shit and needed to shut the fuck up. If she was pregnant, I doubt if it was by my father. After all, in his 40 years on this earth, he had only managed to create me. Qua and Quinn had been calling me like crazy, but I didn't want to speak to either of them. I believed that Qua didn't have anything to do with Rome's murder, but I was just too mentally fucked up right now to deal with a relationship.

Chapter Twenty-Six
QUASIEM 'QUA' SHAKUR

I had Haz hack into Yanni's phone, so I knew that she was in Virginia and never left the address since she had been there. She was ignoring my calls and that shit was pissing me off, but I understood that she had been dealt a fucked-up hand and needed some time to figure that shit out. I was pissed that I hadn't seen my baby girl in a few days though and that was going to have me going to Virginia and dragging her ass home. Currently, me, Haz and Twist were in Baltimore. Apparently, that nigga Niko started running low on money and decided to do a show at some underground spot to make some quick cash. We were in the parking lot parked a few spaces over from his car and waiting for his bitch ass to show his face.

"There that bitch go right there. What the fuck? That nigga must have did one song." Twist said making us laugh.

It was only 11:30 and he was leaving his lil fuck ass performance already. Haz waited until he was damn near out of the parking lot to pull out after him. We followed him about 30 minutes from the club to a run-down ass house in the hood. We parked a couple blocks down and walked back down to the house. As we were walking up, we noticed Kaycie coming out. That bitch knew he was here the whole fuckin time. If she wasn't Yanni's sister I would let Haz put a bullet in her head.

She closed the door, got in her car and drove away. Me and Haz walked up to the front door while Twist went around back. After about three minutes of waiting for Twist to make it to the back of the house, I kicked the door in, and we all rushed inside. Just like we thought Niko tried to go out the back door, but Twist was waiting for his ass with a nine pointed at his head. We forced his ass to the little dining room and made him sit down.

"Well, well, well, if it isn't Niko that put his hands on my boo Quinn, that couldn't take care of his responsibilities as a mother fuckin man." Haz said making me and Twist laugh. This dumb nigga was sitting up here mocking 'Baby Boy' when we're here to kill this nigga.

"I ain't got no beef with y'all niggas. Whatever this is about can be worked out." His bitch ass had the nerve to say.

"This ain't about no street shit nigga; this shit is personal." Haz said opening up the bookbag he was carrying on his back and pulling out a sharp ass butcher knife.

As soon as he saw the knife Niko's pussy ass started to cry. He was a coward just like I figured. I grabbed his right hand and stretched it out on the table while Twist held his body still. One whack of that sharp ass knife and his hand completely detached from his body. Haz started laughing like a maniac and Niko screamed so loud I knew for sure somebody had to have heard his hoe ass. We repeated the process and Haz chopped off the nigga's left hand as well.

"Bet you won't put ya hands on my bitch again." Haz said laughing.

That nigga Niko was in so much pain, he had a look of shock on his face and didn't know which hand to tend to first. That shit was hilarious.

"Please man, please don't kill me." He mumbled; he was getting weaker and weaker because of the amount of blood he was losing.

"Don't please me motherfucka. If you would have pleased ya bitch we wouldn't be here, now would we?" Haz said.

This was his show; me and Twist was just there for the ride.

"Call an ambulance please." Niko cried like a bitch.

"You ain't gonna need an ambulance my boy; the morgue coming for ya ass." Haz said and put a bullet in Niko's head.

Another nigga gone because he wanted to do some hoe shit. We left as quickly as we came. Ditched the stolen car and headed back home. On the ride back, I couldn't help but think about Yanni but if she wanted to play childish ass games, I was going to let her. I had never chased a bitch and I wasn't going to start now. I didn't give a fuck how much I loved her.

Chapter Twenty-Seven
AKACIA 'KAYCIE' MAJORS

I had left Niko's bitch ass in the house so I could go to hospital. I hadn't been feeling good at all and since I wasn't from around here, I opted to go to the ER instead of finding a doctor and all that bullshit. Needless to say, my ass was pregnant, and I was pissed the fuck off. I didn't want no damn kids, but I had fucked around and missed my depo shot because of all that bullshit I had going on. I was only nine weeks, so I knew that the baby was Niko's and he wasn't going to be happy about the shit either. He had told me how he had a daughter with some bitch named Malaysia and he wanted nothing to do with her or the baby.

When I got to the house and walked up to the door I noticed it was slightly open which caused me to panic. Since my father's death, I had been paranoid and carrying a gun in my purse. I pulled the gun out of my bag and slowly entered the house. The living room was empty, but I knew something was wrong. I could feel it. I slowly walked towards the kitchen and when I got there that's when I saw him, hands cut off and laying on the floor with a bullet in his head. I cried and said a quick prayer for him, then I got outta dodge.

It took me four and a half hours to drive from Baltimore down to Virginia Beach. I didn't want to be bothered and that was the only place I could think to come for a peace of mind. When I pulled up and saw Yanni's car I wasn't annoyed. Just surprised that we both had the same thought. It was crazy how much things had changed in a year. If Yanni would have never met Rome we still wouldn't have found out about all the shit that our father had done to us in the name of love. When I walked in the house Yanni jumped up from where she was sitting on the couch like I had scared her. It was almost five am and she was probably asleep.

"It's just me. I didn't know you were here."

"You scared the shit out of me. What are you doing here?" She asked.

"I guess great minds think alike." I said dropping my bags and sitting next to her on the couch.

"How are you feeling?" She asked me.

I had spent most of my life hating my sister because of the love and attention she got from our father. She wanted a relationship and I couldn't give her that because I was so jealous. He seemed to love Yanni unconditionally but now I knew that he never really loved anybody but himself. It was his way or nothing at all and now that he was gone, we would have to figure out how to put the pieces of our lives back together alone. At 19 and 20, how could we do that?

"I'm fucked up. How about you?" I said.

"Same."

"I've been a selfish, evil bitch for as long as I can remember. I have never been a good big sister and I probably still can't be but I swear I will try because as much as I've tried to hate you all this time you are the only family I have ever had and I love you." I said shedding tears.

She wrapped her arms around me, and I hugged my sister back for the first time in a long time.

"I love you, too, and from now on we in this shit together."

"I found Niko dead. I was hiding out with him because I was fucking him before all this shit even happened with Quinn. Now I'm pregnant with his baby. I know it was grimy and fucked up and I'm sorry. I just wanna tell you that now so we won't be trying to build our new relationship on lies." I said.

"I understand now why you have been so hard to love and I'm willing to accept all of the past mistakes as long as we ain't moving like that going forward."

"Is the studio still working in the basement?" I asked.

"Yeah, I went down there the other day."

"So, let's work all this shit out in the booth." I said.

SIX MONTHS LATER

Chapter Twenty-Eight
KIYAN 'YANNI' MAJORS

"We have in the studio today the group Sistah. Akacia and Kiyan have a new EP out that everybody and their mama has been talking about. My favorite song on the EP is "Therapy" and that song speaks to me every single time I hear it."

"AHHHHHHHHH!" Me and Kaycie screamed in Unison as we listened to our interview on The Breakfast Club.

We stayed in Virginia for six months shutting out the outside world and putting all of our hurt and pain into music. We had a bunch of songs but picked seven for the EP and so far, everybody loved it. Our social media presence had tripled, and I was so happy. If somebody would have told me a year ago that I would be jumping full force into the music industry and me and my sister would be best friends I would have laughed in their face.

"So how do you feel about performing at the Music Festival at the waterfront the weekend?" Kaycie asked me.

This was the first time in six months we would be back in NJ and we would be in Jersey City, our hometown. I had mixed emotions about going there. I had left everything behind including my heart. I hadn't seen Qua or even talked to him. After blowing my phone up for a few weeks he stopped. When he finally stopped my heart was broken but I had so much shit going on, so much confusion, so much anger and hurt that I needed to detox and now that I had done that I was scared as fuck that I might see him when I stepped foot in Jersey City. I also hadn't spoken to Quinn, and yeah, I missed her and eventually I forgave her but again I needed to heal alone.

"I'm anxious as fuck. I'm scared to run into Qua and Quinn. Honestly, I'm not ready." I said.

"Girl, I ain't did shit but create enemies so I don't wanna go back to that bitch either." She said and we laughed.

"You've changed. I'm happy for you. Anyway, can you watch Italy for me tonight?"

"Of course, I'll watch my niecy niece. Where you going?"

That's what she called Italy since she was her niece from both sides me and Rome. That was some ghetto shit, but it was what it was.

"Millz taking me out again."

Millz was this rapper I met two months ago. He was a big deal in the DMV area and me and Kaycie hit him up to collab on some work and we had a little connection. It was nothing like the connections I had with Rome and Qua and that's why I liked it because it was easy. Italy crawled over to me and I picked her up and kissed her cheeks. She was the light around me and my sister in our darkest times and if it wasn't for my beautiful baby we probably wouldn't have made. She had a head full of hair that I had pulled up in a curly ponytail, and she was so chubby and beautiful. I was thanking God every day that Rome left me with her.

The television was on and when a news report from Jersey City flashed across the screen I turned the volume up.

"Today the body of 29- year-old Barnard Jones better known as Black was found by a couple walking along side the Hudson River. The pair spotted the mutilated body floating in the water and called police. Barnard was reported missing by his mother six months ago. There are no leads on the case and no arrests have been made at this time." The reporter said.

I closed my eyes and said a quick prayer for Qua Black was the nigga that shot him while I was pregnant with Italy and I knew that he was the person responsible for sending the nigga to an early grave. If I wasn't looking forward to going home a few minutes ago, I damn sure didn't wanna go back now.

$$

The performance was hype! We were only supposed to perform "Therapy" but ended up performing "Love Lost" too. The love was genuine and real, and I was happy I came until we were walking back towards the car and there he was. It seemed like time stopped. I noticed the bitch on his arms but I paid her ass no mind. His dreads were neatly twisted, and he was looking like a whole meal in a Givenchy t-shirt. He cockily walked up to me ignoring Millz and grabbed my face in his hands. He turned my face slightly to the left then right like he was making sure I was unharmed or something before he let me go.

"Wassup Lil Shorty." He spoke.

"Wassup Quasiem." I replied causing a cocky smirk to spread across his lips.

"Long time no see. Funny how you took my fuckin daughter and disappeared. Couldn't answer a fuckin call, send a picture or nothing. You had to be booked for a show to bring ya fuckin ass back to the hood. That's crazy Superstar."

"Right to the point all in front of mixed company. Really Qua."

"You wanna do this shit in private that's cool. Let's fuckin go." He said grabbing my arm and snatching me away from Millz.

"Aye you bugging. Get the fuck off my girl." Millz said.

"Who the fuck you talking to bitch. Get ya lil boyfriend before I slap the shit outta him." Qua said getting in Millz face but I stepped in front of him to defuse the situation.

At this point I was kicking myself for even deciding to stay at the festival with Millz instead of going back to the hotel with Kaycie and Italy.

"Millz, it's cool. I need to talk to him. I'll meet you back at the room." I told.

"I doubt that." Qua said.

He turned to Twist and told him to bring ole girl home. She smacked her teeth and rolled her eyes but didn't say shit to object. I followed behind him with an attitude because I had worked so hard on my zin and shit. A bitch had been singing, doing yoga and I felt at peace, now here go Qua with the drama.

The ride to his house was quiet. When I walked in, I felt at home, which was weird. I hadn't felt like I had a home since my father was killed. Some things were upgraded but for the most part it was the same. I headed towards the living room, but his cocky ass walked right past it and upstairs to the bedroom. I bit my tongue and followed him. I didn't want to argue but I knew that conflict was something that was impossible to avoid when it came to matters of the heart.

He sat at the top of the bed and pulled a rolled blunt from the nightstand and lit it. I stood by the bottom of the bed and just watched him. I loved him so much but I doubt that he would believe me if I spoke those words in this moment.

"You souped me the fuck up, made me fall in love with that little girl, sold me dreams of being a father and then you took her from me. You gotta be a cold-blooded bitch to do some foul ass shit like that. Even if you wanted to call it quits you should have never taken Italy away from me." He told me sincerely.

"I'm sorry, Qua, but I couldn't stay here, not with the shit that I found out, with learning about what really happened to my mother and Rome and then my father's death. I just couldn't be here in this place. I couldn't deal with anything. I was on the verge of breaking and I needed to save me."

"You couldn't have told a nigga that shit. Answered a fuckin phone call. That shit was selfish as fuck. You ain't the only motherfucka going through some shit. Tell me the real reason why you left me. Ya bitch ass pops told you some flaw ass shit about me and you believed the nigga." He yelled at me.

"You don't understand. I got fucked up information about every single person I had ever loved that day. I didn't know if the shit was true or not at first but as the months went by and I started to heal some I realized that you had never lied to me before and I knew you didn't lie to me about that. But I felt like since months had went by and you had already stopped calling that it was too late. I forced myself to move on, made myself believe that I was better off leaving this place and all the people here behind me."

"If you loved me the way I love you, you wouldn't have been able to leave me Lil Shorty. Now you got me up here acting like a bitch arguing about some shit that neither of us can change."

"I do love you, Quasiem. Shit just got complicated at the end and now that so much has happened and so much time has passed, I'm not sure if we can fix it."

"Who that bitch ass nigga you had with you?"

"We're kind of dating." I said causing him to kiss his teeth.

"Fuck that nigga."

"I'm sorry if I hurt you." I told him causing the tears that I was holding to finally fall down my face.

Chapter Twenty-Nine
QUASIEM 'QUA' SHAKUR

There was nothing else to say, so I grabbed her hand and stood her up to face me. I wiped the tears from her eyes and just stared at her. Her brown skin was so smooth and beautiful, her thick hair was up in a bun and I couldn't help but stare at her. My baby was beautiful, her lips were full and pouty, and I couldn't help but to kiss them. She didn't kiss me back at first, but I kept on kissing her and squeezing her fat ass until she finally kissed me back.

I pulled the dress she was wearing over her head and unsnapped her bra, then I laid her down on the bed and took her thongs off throwing them to the floor. I stared down at her and admired her perfect body. She had just given birth less than a year ago and it didn't even look like she had ever bear a child. I quickly came out of my clothes and got on top of her kissing all over her body until I was face to face with my favorite part of her. I sucked on her clit and she instantly moaned. I tongue kissed her pussy so good that she was cumming in less than five minutes. I stuck two fingers inside of her and sucked on her clit harder. She tried to push my head away from her but I wouldn't let her. I attacked her clit with my tongue and fucked her with my fingers until she was squirting all over my face. I kissed the front of her pussy and then her stomach and all the way up her body until our lips met again. I stared into her eyes and I could see that she was still in a lot of pain. I pushed my 11 inches into her never taking my eyes off her.

"I'm sorry baby. I swear to God, Qua. I promise you I won't ever hurt you again. Tell me you forgive me." She said to me as I sped up the pace and fucked her harder. I bit her neck and put her legs in the crook of my arms.

"Damn this pussy wet for Daddy." I whispered against her lips.

She moaned out loud with her eyes closed.

"Open ya fuckin eyes. Look at me when I'm talking to you."

She opened her eyes and tears rolled down the sides of her face.

I stroked her hard hitting that spot over and over again. I

had her ass cumming back to back as her pussy was talking to me with each stroke I was giving her.

"I'm cumming again, don't stop."

"Fuck, I missed this good ass pussy. Who pussy is this Kiyan?"

Her legs were shaking like crazy and she was wet as hell. I missed the shit out this pussy. Me and Yanni's sex life had always been perfect. No matter what we went through this part of our relationship was always flawless. She arched her back and opened her legs wider; I massaged her clit while she squeezed her nipples.

"This is your pussy Daddy, you know that."

"Cum on your dick baby. I'm cumming with you." I said as my strokes became shorter and harder. I felt her cum again and I exploded inside of her. I laid next to her and pulled her closer to me kissing her on her neck. After laying in silence for a while I spoke.

"Italy don't even know me; that shit crazy. You be having that fuck nigga around her?" I asked.

I had just got finished fuckin the shit outta her and now it was back to matter at hand.

"No Millz has never really been around her. He's never held or spent any real time with her. He's only ever seen her in passing." She told me.

"Yeah ight." I said sitting up lighting the tip of the blunt again.

"Do you wanna see her?"

"I don't know about that Yanni. You might let me get to know her again and then run the fuck off when shit get a little real."

She tried to get up from the bed, but I pulled her back down. She folded her arms across her chest, but I didn't give a fuck about that shit. Yanni was the first woman I had ever loved. I didn't even believe I loved my mother. Shit was crazy.

I had been doing any and everything for her only for her to get ghost on a nigga in the end. That shit had me pissed the day she left, and I was even more pissed looking at her now because the bitch had the audacity to leave a nigga like me.

"That's not fair of you to say Qua."

"Go to sleep Kiyan cuz you ain't going no fuckin where." I told her.

She had me pissed but if she thought I was letting her go again she was stupid. Once she was sleep, I took her phone and texted Kaycie. Telling her that Twist was going to pick up Italy from her and bring her to Yanni. That hoe Kaycie was all over the radio talking about how much she had changed but I would have to see that shit to believe it and until then that hoe would not know where I laid my head. It took Twist an hour to bring me the baby.

"Good looking Bro." I told him.

"You know I got you." He said before leaving the house.

Italy was up and looking at a nigga strange as fuck, but she didn't cry. I sat in the living room with her watching girly ass cartoons until she fell back to sleep in my arms. I didn't know if I wanted to get attached again but I knew that since I watched her come into this world, I had a connection with Italy. I loved her like my own and that would never change. The next morning, I woke up still in the recliner with Italy sleep on my chest and Yanni standing over us with her phone in her hand taking pictures.

"Get outta here with that shit." I told her playfully.

"When did you get her." She asked taking the baby out of my arms and kissing her cheek.

"I had Twist bring her last night. You don't mind, do you? I was once her father and shit." I said and she rolled her eyes.

"I'm not about to argue with you. I gotta go. I have a photo shoot today and then I'm heading back home." She told me.

"And where is home?"

"New York for right now. We thinking about moving to LA in the next few months though. Listen, I don't want to take Italy away from you, honestly. I feel like shit for taking her away from you. I love you and I don't know what last night was about but..."

Before she could finish the doorbell rang and I went to open the door; it was Sienna.

"What I tell you about popping up at my house without a fuckin invitation?"

"So, you just ditch me to run off with that bitch and then ignore all my calls and texts? Where they do that shit at?"

I had been fuckin with Si for the last few months. I had told myself that I wouldn't fuck with her on that level again, but Si was familiar, and I could trust her which is why I was right back in her pussy when Yanni pissed me off and left town.

"This ain't a good time Si. I'll get up with you later?" I told her.

"No, you'll get up with me now Quasiem." She said walking pass me into the house.

When she saw Yanni holding the baby she stopped walking and turned to face me with tears in her eyes.

"We'll talk about this shit later." I said to her.

"Fuck you Qua." She said and left out of the house slamming my fuckin door in the process.

"So, you back fuckin with her?" Yanni asked.

"Does it fuckin matter?"

"You fucked me raw last night. I think it does." She replied.

"She's a friend."

"Whatever Qua. I'm about to go."

"You want me to kiss ya ass or some shit? I'm not the one that left." I told her.

"You don't have to kiss my ass Qua. You don't have to do shit. As a matter of fact you be with that hoe and I'll be with Millz. I'm not about to play with you. In the meantime, you can see and get Italy anytime you want."

$$

"She ain't ask about me?" Quinn said as soon as I walked into her and Haz's house.

"Naw but you should call her." I replied.

She walked out of the front room leaving me and Haz alone.

"So Wassup y'all fix shit or what?" He asked.

"Naw more like argued, fucked and argued some more. Shit ain't going to work out. Yanni want a nigga to kiss her spoiled ass."

"Cut that girl some slack. I don't think she meant to question your loyalty. I just think that after all that happened, she was fucked up about it and had to get away. It wasn't about you. Now that she's good and she's back around y'all should at least give the shit a real shot." Haz said.

"Nigga you wanna be Dr. Phil so fuckin bad." I said to him.

"What can I say? A nigga like a ghetto savant." I laughed at that shit because it was the truth.

This nigga was killer, drug dealer, went to church on Sunday, could sing, hacked computers and always had some good advice. I appreciated having his ass on my team.

"You ain't never lied about that shit."

Chapter Thirty
QUINN ISSACS

"Baby, I know you got business to handle but can you take the day off. I wanna spend time with you."

"Come on now baby. You know ain't no days off." He said putting a bunch of stacks of money in the safe in our bedroom and closing it.

Needless to say, when I got out of the hospital, I never did get my own apartment. I moved in with Haz and finally found my forever love. He was everything I could have wished for and more. I loved him so much and I was happy to have him in my life. When I was released from the hospital, I wasn't 100 % healed but he was patient and attentive and nursed me back to health. I was happy for the first time in a long time and the only thing that was missing was my best friend.

"Please." I opened my robe exposing my naked body and he came closer to me kissing my lips and palming my ass.

"Damn baby you ain't playing fair." He said to me while he parted my lower lip and rubbed my clit causing my juices to flow.

I got down on my knees and freed his dick from the jeans he was wearing taking him into my mouth and sucking him just how he liked. I hated to suck Niko's dick but with Haz I loved it. Giving head hit different when you know for a fact you the only bitch he fuckin. I made the head extra sloppy and had him cumming in my mouth in no time.

"I love you Hassan." I said to him.

"I love you too." He said causing tears to fall from my eyes.

It was the first time he had said those words to me and although I knew by his actions that he loved me, to hear him say it felt so damn good.

He removed the rest of his clothes and laid me back on the bed. I wrapped my legs around his waist and stared at him not believing that this was happening to me. He entered me and the passion in his stroke had me cumming almost instantly. I made love to my man for a few hours before we showered together and got dressed.

We were on our way to Benihana but Haz had to make a quick stop in the hood.

"Stay in the car. I'll be right back." He told me.

I plugged up my phone so I could listen to Yanni's EP when all of a sudden, a damn brick came flying through the windshield. I screamed and covered my face from the glass that had fallen all around me. When I got myself together and looked up, I saw that hoe Meesha standing in front of Haz's car with a smirk on her face. I flew out the car so fast and started beating that hoe ass when her dirty ass friend Stacy jumped in. Haz came running out of the building and damn near tossed that bitch Stacy in the air. She hit the ground with a loud thud and didn't dare get the fuck back up again. Haz pulled me off of Meesha and pushed her ass back.

"What the fuck is ya problem?"

"Nigga you my fucking problem. You left me to be with this big-headed hoe and thought I wasn't going to handle the bitch when I finally caught up with her." Her dusty ass had the nerve to say.

"I left cuz I caught you eating a bitch pussy, but I guess you forgot about that shit. Get ya dumb ass the fuck away from me before I send you to ya maker." Haz growled.

I had never seen him so mad.

"I been homeless since you left and you walking around shining like shit sweet. Since when you stopped taking care of ya responsibilities Hassan." She cried.

I kind of felt bad for the simple hoe.

"You ain't his fuckin responsibility. McDonalds hiring hoe. Get off ya fishy ass and get a job." I yelled.

"Get in the car baby." Haz said to me and I did what I was told. I was pissed as I brushed glass from the seats.

"You should feel fucked up for having me out her struggling when you got it Haz." She cried, forcing me to roll my damn eyes.

"You ain't my responsibility Meesha. The whole fuckin time we were together I tried to get ya dumb ass to get ya

GED, take some classes or even get a fuckin job. You don't wanna do shit but chase behind this bucket head bitch so let that bitch give you a place to stay. You had somewhere to rest ya head at, the bills was paid for five months and that was more than enough time for you to at least try to find a job but ya dizzy ass ain't do shit but sit on ya ass hoping that another motherfucka was going to pay ya way. I don't owe you shit."

"How could you do this to me Haz. I loved you. I tried to give you all that I had, and it wasn't good enough for you. We lost our first child together and you told me you would always be there for me, but you lied. You left me to grieve and figure shit out all on my own. You weren't there so how could you be mad when I found other shit to help me cope." Meesha was hysterical now. I could tell that what she was saying was getting to Haz, but he didn't reply.

He just turned around and got in the car.

"What baby?" I asked.

"I don't wanna talk about that shit."

One thing about Haz was that he was so chill and laid back, but he would shut the fuck down on you in a minute. We pulled up to the house and I got out the car.

"You not coming in."

"I'll be back later."

I was so fuckin annoyed at this point; the Yanni shit was on my mind heavy since I found out that she was in town and all I wanted to do was spend the day up under my man til that dirty bitch had to ruin it for me. I sat on the porch swing and pulled my phone from my Chanel bag. I called Yanni and waited for her to answer. When she did, I was so shocked I didn't know what to say.

"Oh, um I wasn't expecting you to answer honestly. How are you doing Kiyan?"

"I'm ok. I was going to text you anyway and invite you to lunch; it's a lot of shit we need to talk about."

"I'm free whenever you ready."

"Cool so meet me at Jus Be Claws in an hour."

$$

When I walked in the restaurant and saw Akacia, I swear I wanted to walk right the fuck back out. If it wasn't for me wanting my best friend back, I would have but I continued to the table and took a seat.

"Hey y'all."

"Hey. I know you probably wondering why I'm here, but I really wanted to come and apologize to you."

"For what? We've had our differences, but you haven't done anything directly to me."

"Actually, I did. I fucked Niko and when he stabbed you, I went to Baltimore to be with him. I ultimately ended up getting pregnant but decided to get an abortion. I've changed. I'm not the same Kaycie and being that you are my sister's best friend I would like for you to forgive me Quinn."

I was pissed. I wanted to slap the shit out of that grimy bitch.

"Wow, that's real fucked up. I don't know if I can forgive that." I said.

"Why? You went and moved in with Niko even after you found out that he and my father plotted to have Rome killed." Yanni spoke up.

I thought about if for a while and she was right. I knew better than anyone how easy it was for Niko to manipulate any situation. He was a puppet master and knew how to control.

"You're right. I did do some fucked up shit when I was with Niko. I know how easy it is to be used by him and for that I will forgive you Kaycie. I can't lie and hearing interviews and listening to the music does show you've changed a lot."

"Good because even though we weren't friends we've know each other since we were kids and I just wanna rebuild." Kaycie said.

"I also want to apologize again Yanni. I should have told you and let you do what you saw fit with the information. Niko was beating my ass and I was so scared of what he would do if he found out that I told. I'm sorry. I should have never betrayed you in that way." I sincerely said.

"I know Quinn and it took me a while, but I understand and I'm not mad. The people responsible got their Karma and I can move on from that." She said. We all got up and hugged before enjoying a seafood feast. I felt good to have my friend back and I just hoped that with time our friendship would be as strong as it was before.

Chapter Thirty-One
HASSAN 'HAZ' SHAHID

When I left Quinn, I went and got my fuckin windshield fixed. By the time I got my car fixed and handled some business it was nine at night. I can't lie and say that Meesha's situation wasn't fuckin with a nigga. I was with her for three years and at one point I loved her so of course I didn't want to see her in the streets, but I didn't want to be burdened by the bitch either. I was surprised that she brought up our daughter. It was something that neither of us liked to talk about which is why that situation was left hidden deep inside and unhealed. After we had been together a little over two years Meesha gave birth to my daughter India. She was born stillborn and that shit was the hardest thing that I had ever had to go through in my life. I hadn't forgot about my baby girl, but I did forget that I wasn't the only person who lost her.

Meesha had carried my child in her womb for nine months and had to give birth to her lifeless body. She was never the same after that and was probably one of the reasons why she shut down. We both shut down and eventually we were past the point of fixing the relationship. I was just ready to let the shit go. As a man I should have put more effort into making sure she was ok, but I didn't know how to do that when I wasn't ok after that shit. This information didn't change how I felt about Meesha. I was done with her, but I would try to be understanding.

I pulled up in front of Stacy's house and just like I thought her and Meesha were on the porch. She had her real hair up in a bun and I laughed cuz I knew that shit was killing her. Meesha had a head full of hair but the bitch loved weave. I blew the horn and she came walking over to the car and got in. I pulled off as soon as she was inside.

"I should slap the shit outta you, but my girl already fucked you up, so I'll let it slide."

"Haz if you came to rub that bitch in my face you can let me the fuck out."

"Watch ya mouth. You know I don't do that disrespectful shit."

"What you want Hassan?"

"Look, I'm sorry I wasn't there after India. I was just so fucked up and I was trying to be strong and deal with what I was going through that I forgot to make sure you were good too. This doesn't mean that we can be together again; it just means that I know I dropped the ball and I acknowledge that shit. You gotta get ya shit together though Mesh. Yeah, we were together for years, but I don't owe you shit. You need to move the fuck on. Let go." I told her pulling up to a two-family house in Bayonne.

I used the key to get inside. Meesha looked around before sitting down on the couch.

"Who lives here?" She asked.

"You do. I paid the rent for a year so you good. It's fully furnished but let me make myself clear after this I'm done. You need to get a fuckin job and stack some bread so that when this year is up you can take care of yaself. I did my part and after this you on your own." I said.

Meesha cried for a while before coming over to me and hugging.

"Thanks, Haz. I swear I'll do what I have to do. The breakup was hard on me but I gotta let you go so that I can move on with my life."

I left Meesha's house and headed home. Dealing with her ass had me drained. I didn't tell Meesha the whole truth. That rental property was one of many that I owned. After the year was up if she was working and handling her business, I would allow her to continue to stay there but if her ass didn't take this shit serious and get it together, I would put her ass right back on the streets.

When I got home, Quinn was in the bedroom. She was crying and looked pissed about something.

"What's the matter baby?" I asked her not really in the mood to be dealing with no dumb shit.

She opened her phone and handed it to me. It was a video that hoe Stacy had taken of Meesha getting in my car.

"So, you left me earlier to go be with that bitch." She asked.

"You see clear as day that video was taken not too long ago so stop acting stupid. I was going to tell you."

"Tell me what?"

I put Meesha up in an apartment for a year to give her a chance to get on her feet." I said taking off my clothes.

"Why the fuck would you do that shit unless you still love that bitch." She said sounding insecure.

"If I loved Meesha I wouldn't be here with you."

"So why you worrying about what she got going on? You ain't been worrying about that hoe."

"You right but she mentioned some things today that made a nigga feel bad. She gave birth to my stillborn daughter and I didn't know how to handle that shit myself so I dropped the ball when I didn't make sure that she was straight. I'm not making excuses but I'm saying I understand more now that the shit we was going through when we were together was a result of the child we loss and the unhealed trauma from it. I put her up in an apartment and told her that this is the last time I'mma look out for her."

"Wow you really on some other shit and you did all this without telling me." She said.

"I'mma man, Quinn. I don't have to tell shit. The shit is done, and I would appreciate if you drop that shit cuz I'm not in the mood to be arguing with you right now. She carried a child for me. I should have been made sure she was straight, but I didn't. I don't want Mesh and after tonight I'm done with her so it ain't no need for us to keep talking about that shit."

I took a shower and when I came out Quinn was sitting on the bed phone in hand with a mean mug on her pretty ass face. I wasn't one for negative energy and I could feel the anger pouring off her. I walked over to her and pulled her by her leg to the edge of the bed.

"Stop Haz. I'm not in the mood." She whined.

"Shut the fuck up." I told her pulling her panties off. She looked good as fuck in my wife beater with her nipples showing through the thin fabric.

I opened her legs wide and licked her clit. I could feel the attitude leaving her body. I put my face in her pussy and ate her like it was the best thing I had ever tasted. I sucked on her clit hard then licked it softly putting two fingers into her slippery wet opening. I felt her pussy squeezing my fingers tight and knew she was about to cum, so I removed my finger and stood up.

"What are you doing?" She whined.

"Naw you mad about some bullshit. I'm about to go make a few runs."

"Haz, I'm not fuckin playing with you." She snapped.

"You still mad about that bitch?"

"No, I'm not mad." She whined like a spoiled brat.

"You still sound mad to me."

"Baby, I'm not mad. Come here."

"For what? What you want?" I asked teasing her.

"I want you."

"Want me to what? Say that shit."

"I want you to come over here and finish eating my pussy. I want you to make me cum." She whined opening her legs again giving me a clear view of my favorite place in the world.

"Nasty ass." I said to her as I walked over to her and tongue kissed her pussy once again.

She wrapped her legs around my neck and moaned out loud when I stuck one finger in her pussy and one in her ass while I sucked on her clit.

"Dammit Haz what are you doing to me?" She asked

damn near screaming as I continued to assault every hole. Soon she was squirting all over my face and I was licking up every drop.

"Ok, ok I can't take it anymore." She screamed out. I got up and laid on top of her. Sliding my dick deep inside of her while I kissed her lips.

She sucked on my lips greedily tasting her own juices. I kissed her neck and then her ear while stroking her slowly. Her legs were shaking, and she kept cumming back to back letting me know that I was doing my job.

"I don't want no insecure bitch. I ain't that other nigga. I'm not going to hurt you, Quinn, but you gotta trust me." I whispered in her ear while I continued to make love to her.

"I do trust you and I love you." She said.

"Well act like it then."

I fucked Quinn until I was weak in the knees. Afterwards we laid in bed together, the TV watching us cuz we weren't paying that shit no mind.

"I'm sorry about your daughter." She said while laying on my chest.

"It's cool. I'm good now."

"Do you want more kids?"

"Yeah eventually."

"What we have is just so amazing. I've never felt this way about anybody before or even had anybody to feel this way about me. It's like I'm so happy with you and that scares the shit outta me because I can't lose you." She said and kissed my chest.

I rubbed my hands through her hair and kissed her forehead.

"Baby, I was with Meesha for three years and what I felt for her was nothing close to what I feel for you. You got me and I ain't going nowhere." I promised her.

"Good because I can't handle another heart break. I just can't wait to grow old with you and give you a bunch of babies."

"I'mma hold you to that shit too."

"I got you onna gang." She said laughing.

Chapter Thirty-Two
AKACIA 'KAYCIE' MAJORS

I know y'all probably thinking a bitch faking and I ain't really changed shit but after pulling that trigger and killing the only father I had ever known and then finding Niko's dead body plus realizing that all the family I had was dead except for my sister and my niece a bitch did a whole 180. I had to mentally detox and going to that house in Virginia and finding my sister there was the best thing that could have happened to me. We disconnected from the world, allowed ourselves to hit rock bottom, and then we built each other back up again all while putting every fuckin thing into the music.

It was a hard, devastating process but the end result was amazing. I realized that my sister was the most important person in my life and that I would never take her for granted again. Deciding to kill Niko's child was also hard but I had to do it. I couldn't bring that baby into this world in the midst of my storm; it wouldn't have been fair. Currently, I was in front of my Aunt Janine's house; she was also family and I had done some bullshit to her. Although Kev was mostly to blame because he was an adult, I felt the need to come by and apologize. It was all a part of this healing journey I was on to be a better me.

I rang her bell and when she answered I was shocked at what I saw. Her hair was all over her head, and she smelled like stale liquor and musk. Her brown skin was dry, she had huge bags under her eyes, and she looked dull and lifeless. I looked around her into the house, and I smelled the mess before I saw it.

"What the fuck are you doing here Kaycie?"

"I just came to check on you and to say how sorry I am for all that I put you through." She rolled her eyes at me and laughed causing me to want to throw up at the smell of her breath.

"Bitch, you fucked my man for years behind my back." She slurred.

"I know and I was wrong and I'm not making excuses, but he came onto me and offered me a lot of money. At the time I was just being wild and having fun."

"So, where is he? He's been missing for months and I know you probably know something about that shit."

I did know where he was. I had witnessed my father kill him but in the state of mind she was in I knew that she wouldn't be able to handle that information.

"I heard but I don't know where he is. The last time I saw him was when my Daddy found out about us. Look, I know you're mad, but do you need anything?" I asked.

"Your Daddy? You mean my only brother who you killed in cold blood. I hate you bitch, and I curse the day you were born. You took everything away from and I'll hate you as long as I live." She said and I knew she meant every word because I could feel the hate.

"I'm sorry you feel that way Aunt Janine, but I respect your wishes." I said and turned to walk away.

"You just came here to rub your success in my face you little whore. Your sister was supposed to let me adopt her child and changed her mind at the last minute. My brother told me all about how she refused to give me the child that was rightfully mine. I hate both of y'all hoes and y'all better hope that I never see either one of y'all hoes again." She yelled at my back as I made my way to my car. She was as crazy as her damn brother.

"Baby, you home?" I called out when I finally reached my condo in New York.

"In here." Chris called out.

Chris was a producer that I met while still in Virginia trying to put the finishing touches on our EP. He was the opposite of everything I had ever been attracted to and I loved him for that. This man had made me feel so loved in the short amount of time we had been together, and I was honored to be his wife. Yes, y'all heard right. After only three months of dating we flew to Vegas and got married. We hadn't announced it to the world yet and only Yanni and Millz knew but we were so happy and so in love.

"I missed you babe." I told him kissing his lips.

"What you do today?" He asked.

"Me and Yanni had lunch with her best friend. I was able to apologize for the whole Niko situation, then we had a photoshoot. After that, we separated, and I ended up going to see my Aunt to apologize for fuckin her husband.... Oh my God, babe, saying this shit out loud is embarrassing." I said shaking my head.

Chris just came over to me and kissed my lips. He knew every detail about my past and had never judged me for any of it, and I loved him for that shit.

"The past doesn't define who you are now. You know that Akacia. How did it go with your Aunt?"

"Not so good. She was dirty and the house was dirty as fuck too. That's not like my Aunt at all. I mean her husband is dead and her only brother is dead; she's all alone. I'm worried about her, but she made it clear that she doesn't want anything to do with me or my sister." I said feeling bad for the situation she was in. I prayed that she would be able to snap out of it and get her life back on track. If she ever needed me for anything, I would be there for her with bells on.

"You can only offer the apology. You can't force her to accept it so don't go beating yourself up about it."

"I know babe."

Chapter Thirty-Three
KIYAN 'YANNI' MAJORS

I had a long ass day. I left Italy with Qua and I told him I would pick her up in the morning. When he found out that I was doing lunch with the girls then I had a photoshoot he refused to let me "drag her around with me all day" as he called it. I was used to taking Italy everywhere with me because I didn't trust her with anybody but Kaycie. Now that Qua and Quinn was back in our lives, I was looking forward to having help with my little Queen. I entered my bedroom and almost had a damn heart attack. Millz was sitting on my bed looking crazy as fuck.

"What the fuck are you doing here Kamil? You scared the shit outta me. How did you even get in?" I asked him. We didn't live together.

"The door man let me in. Is that a problem?"

"Yes, you should have called." I told him.

"I did call. You ain't answer and you ain't been home since yesterday so wassup with that?"

"I ended up staying at Qua's. We were talking about the baby and time just got away from us. Then I had to work today."

Out of nowhere, Millz grabbed me by my throat and slammed me up against the wall. He was the jealous type always questioning me even though we weren't that serious in my mind, but he had never put his hands on me. I slapped the shit out of him, and he tossed me on the bed and pried my legs open. I screamed not sure of what the fuck he was about to do. Panic set in and I started kicking but he was too strong for me. He reached under the Chanel t-shirt dress I was wearing and snatched my panties off. He took his fingers and shoved them inside of me and then brought them to his face to smell. After his inspection of my private area he let me go and I laid there and cried. I couldn't believe he had done that shit. I never even had sex with Millz; he had eaten me out a few times but that was that so I couldn't believe the audacity of this nigga.

"Get the fuck outta my house Kamil!" I screamed.

"Why, so you can go fuck ya baby daddy? I ain't going nowhere!" He yelled back at me.

"You got me fucked up." I said.

"No bitch you got me fucked up. I been wining and dining ya spoiled ass and this the thanks I fuckin get. You going to give me some pussy tonight." He said.

I started going crazy kicking and screaming. I still had on my Chanel sneakers and managed to kick him in the stomach. He doubled over and I tried to run but he tripped me causing me to fall to the floor. He flipped me over and got on top of me.

"Letting a nigga eat on ya pussy and shit but go fuck another nigga. You stupid ass bitch. The fuck type of bitch ass nigga you take me for."

He put all his weight on me to keep me from going anywhere while he struggled to free his little pencil dick.

"Kamil, please stop! Please, I'm sorry."

He grabbed my hands holding them above my head and bent down to kiss me, but I turned my face and his lips landed on my neck. I would have never dreamed that Kamil was this type of person.

"I'm about to be up in this pussy all night."

Tears fell from my eyes and I cried hard because I couldn't believe this shit was about to happen to me yet again. I felt his dick at the opening of my vagina, and I started to get hysterical. I felt like that 12-year-old girl that was getting her innocence stolen again. I squeezed my eyes shut tight and suddenly I heard a small POP sound and Kamil dropped on top of me. I screamed and turned my head to see Qua standing behind me with a smoking gun. He ran over to me and pushed Kamil's lifeless body off me. I looked down and saw the hole between his eyes and I didn't feel bad at all. I couldn't believe I had spent months getting to know him and he was a sick monster. Qua helped me up and I fell into his arms crying.

"You ok? You good?" He asked.

I shook my head because that's all I could manage to do.

He picked up his phone and told someone he needed a cleaning service and then gave my address.

"Come on, let's get outta here."

On the ride back to his house, I cried the entire time but when we pulled up, I started to calm down. I had always felt safe here and like I said it was the only home I had ever known. Once inside I realized Italy wasn't there.

"Where is Italy?" I asked.

I stood in the bathroom while Qua ran a bath for me.

"I had Quinn come and get her so I could track ya ass down and drag you home. We separated for six months. I'm not letting you go again. Fuck that. You wanna tell me what happened?"

"When I got home, he was there waiting. Said my door man let him up. He was mad cuz he knew that I had stayed the night with you last night. He snatched off my panties and shoved his fingers inside of me saying how I hadn't fucked him yet, but I fucked you and all this other crazy shit. He tried to rape me, but you didn't let him." I said without crying. I was tired of tears.

"I'mma kill ya doorman cuz that nigga let me upstairs too." He said seriously.

"If he hadn't you wouldn't have been able to save me."

"I'll never let another person hurt you again. You got my word on that Lil Shorty."

"You have always been there when I needed you. I don't know why I felt like it would be different after my father died. I shouldn't have left you." I said emotional.

"You had to so that you could find yaself. Look at you, a superstar and shit. Doing photoshoots and interviews and shit."

"Have you even listened to the music."

"Every day since it came out."

"You know you gotta get in the booth and do a song with me right?"

"I got you. I'mma have to charge you but I got you." He said and I laughed.

"How's your mother?"

"Surprisingly, still clean. I got her a house and I take care of her financially, but we don't have much of a relationship. I seen her a few times since she got out of rehab but that's it." He said washing me up.

"You only get one mother; try to make it work."

"You sound like Haz with all the Dr. Phil bullshit."

$$

A week later we had the grill going and the music playing in the back yard while we all got back reacquainted. It was like no time had passed at all. Me, Qua, Kaycie, Chris, Quinn, Haz, Twist, Capri their daughter Tyana, Italy and even Qua's mother Natalie all ate, laughed and had a good time. I was sitting with the women gossiping when all of a sudden, I heard singing in my ear. I turned around and my man was singing "Let's Get Married" by Jagged Edge. I knew that Qua could sing his ass off from us being in the studio together before, but he had told me that he hated to sing. Thought it made him look soft but there was nothing soft about my baby.

Tears came to my eyes and I smiled because I knew that this man would do any and everything for me. He had taken me in when my father turned his back on me. He went through an entire pregnancy and delivery with me. Took on the role of a father and boyfriend and even though it was all new to him he conquered it all. He loved me unconditionally with no limits and had proved that to me over and over again. He allowed me back into his life after I ran from him, and here he was down on one knee singing to me, wanting to make me his wife.

"You got me out here doing this sucka ass singing and shit, but I love you and I just want to spend the rest of my life keeping that smile on your face. I didn't know what love was until you showed me. I didn't even think I was capable of putting somebody else's well-being before my own but now I know that I would die for you and my baby girl. You changed mem Kiyan. You made me want to be a better man. Hurting you has never even crossed my mind. I'm yours, I'm on your team, I move for you, I breathe for you, my loyalty, my love, this dick, all for you shorty. Will you marry me Kiyan?" Everybody laughed and I couldn't hold back the tears if I tried.

"Yes, Quasiem Shakur, I'll marry you." I said. He placed a five Carat diamond ring on my finger, and everybody applauded while my husband-to-be kissed my lips and held me tight.

"I love you so much." He said.

"I love you more."

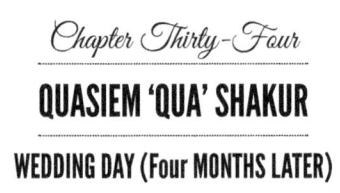

Chapter Thirty-Four
QUASIEM 'QUA' SHAKUR
WEDDING DAY (Four MONTHS LATER)

I knocked Yanni's ass up and she was currently three months pregnant. She wanted to hurry up and get married before she started showing and her wish was my command.

We were in the groom's room in the church waiting to be called. We all had on Armani Tuxedos and red bottom shoes.

A nigga was looking sharp as fuck waiting to see my bride. I had Haz and Twist by my side as always and I wished that my brother could be here with me. It was a bittersweet feeling and I would forever miss his presence in moments like these.

"I'm proud of you bro." Twist said to me giving me a hug.

"Me too kid." Haz said, following suit.

"I never thought I would see the day I would be getting married. Shit crazy."

The door opened and my mother came inside the room and hugged me. We had been working on repairing our relationship. I can't say it wasn't hard to forgive but Yanni was right. I only had one mother and I couldn't hold her mistakes against her forever. She got clean and she never stopped trying to earn my forgiveness so the only thing I could do was let all that shit go and start fresh.

"I'm so happy for you baby. Yanni is incredible. I know she'll take good care of ya heart." She said to me.

"Thanks Ma. I'm glad you're here."

"Y'all let's go; they getting ready to start."

I stood at the alter next to Pastor Andrews waiting to see my wife in that fifteen-thousand-dollar dress she just had to have. Haz walked down the aisle with Quinn and Twist walked down with Kaycie. They walked down to the band playing and when Kaycie reached the front of the church she started singing "With You" by Tony Terry.

When I'm with you, I hear a song
That makes me laugh and smile and sing to you
When I'm with you, I feel so free
I feel that love is going to take control of me

When I saw Yanni walking down the aisle in her wedding dress a nigga was fighting back tears. I was mesmerized with her she was so beautiful. My eyes locked with hers and I knew I was the luckiest man in the world. It was so crazy. I had known her most of her life but never even paid attention to her. That day I walked into O's office, it was like I was seeing her for the first time and since then I had been deeply in love with her. Even when I fought not to let it show it always did.

When she got to the front of the church, I reached out my hand and helped her up the single step that led to the alter. I lifted her veil and the tears that I had been trying so hard to fight came sliding down my face. Whoever said thugs don't cry was a mother fuckin lie cuz looking into my wife's eyes on this day made it impossible for me not to shed a tear a two. She reached out and wiped my face.

"I love you." She said to me.

"I love you more."

"Most people have the definition of love all wrong. 1 Corinthians 13:4-7 says Love is patient, love is kind. It does not envy, it does not boast, it is not proud. It does not dishonor others, it is not self-seeking, it is not easily angered, it keeps no record of wrongs. Love does not delight in evil but rejoices with the truth. It always protects, always trusts, always hopes, always perseveres. Love never fails. In times of trouble remember to love before anything else. Quasiem, your vows." The Pastor said.

"I had known you for years but when I walked into O's office that day it was like I was seeing you for the first time. I saw your pain even though you were smiling, and I had this instinct to protect you. I felt possessive and that was new for me. I knew from that moment on that I was yours. I was at your beck and call ready to fight for you, ready to go to war for you, ready to risk it all just to see you smile. From that day on, I knew that everything that had happened prior to that day happened so that I could stand here before you and God and pledge my life and love to you. I will do anything just to see that smile on your face. You bring out the best in me. You've shown me parts of myself that I didn't even know existed. You make me better baby. You make me want to be better and I'll live the rest of my life cherishing you and all that we will build together."

She was crying and fuckin up her makeup.

"That day in my Dad's office I felt it to. It was like a magnet pulling me closer and closer to you and, at first, I was so scared because I had been so hurt but you healed what I thought couldn't be healed. And when I thought that I could never love again you showed me a love that I have never known. God sent you to me because he knew that you were the missing piece of my heart that I had been looking so hard for. Because of you I grew a strength that I didn't even know I had. With you I feel invincible like I can do anything... be anything because I know that you have my back and that you'll ride for me through whatever. I feel so complete with you and I will spend the rest of my life showing you how grateful I am for you and how much I love you."

"Do you take Kiyan Aliyah Majors as your lawful wife, to have and to hold, from this day forward, for better or for worse, for richer or for poorer, in sickness and in health, to love and cherish until death do you part?"

"I do." I said.

"Do you take Quasiem Kamer Shakur as your lawful husband, to have and to hold, from this day forward, for better or for worse, for richer or for poorer, in sickness and in health, to love and cherish until death do you part?"

"I do." She said.

"By the power vested in me, I now pronounce you man and wife. You may kiss the bride."

I kissed Yanni with so much passion my dick was hard, and I was ready to say fuck that reception and take her ass back to the room. As we were about to jump the broom her Aunt Janine came out of one of the pews with a gun in her hand.

"I told you I would kill you!" She screamed and before anyone could even react, she shot Akacia in the chest.

Pandemonium broke out and all the guests started running towards the door. Trampling over one another to get out of the church. D-Cash tackled the crazy bitch and snatched the gun out of her hand.

"Noooooo!" Yanni screamed to the top of her lungs as she ran over to her sister.

She pulled Kaycie into her lap, blood staining the white dress she wore. I was in shock; I hadn't even known that Janine was a threat. If I would have known the bitch would have been dead.

"Kaycie, please don't leave me like this. Please Kaycie. I can't take another loss, you know that. Fight. Somebody call an ambulance!" She cried hysterically hugging her sister.

"I love you Yanni." Kaycie struggled to say,. She was choking on her own blood and tears were falling from her eyes. Her husband kissed her lips and she smiled up at him.

"Don't give up Kaycie. Please don't do this. My heart can't take it, please. I need you here with me. I love you so much please!"

My wife cried and pleaded with her sister not to leave her. She kissed her on the cheek and the ambulance rushed down the aisle and loaded her on the stretcher. I took Yanni in my arms and held her tight. I prayed that Kaycie made it. I knew how close they had gotten, and I hated that the happiest day of our lives had turned into a tragedy.

KIYAN 'YANNI' MAJORS
ONE YEAR LATER

We were in the back yard surrounded by family as we released purple balloons into the sky in honor of Akacia's one-year anniversary in heaven. My sister didn't make it after being shot at my wedding. I held my five-month-old son Quasiem Jr. in my arms and was grateful to have him here. I had almost miscarried when my sister died but through the grace of God and with the strength of my husband holding me together while I was falling apart, I was able to get through it. Of course, it was still one of the biggest losses I had taken but I was taking it day by day. Whenever I listened to our music, I would cry like a baby, but it also made me feel close to her.

Before she passed, she was at peace. She changed her life around and had tried to make amends with those she had hurt but unfortunately Aunt Janine wasn't trying to hear that. She had lost a lot and unfairly she blamed it all on Kaycie. She never blamed her husband for sleeping with her underage niece and she didn't blame my father for lying to her and promising her a child that wasn't his to promise to her in the first place. She needed someone to be responsible for her grief and my sister paid for that with her life.

Aunt Janine had been arrested and was facing life in prison when she was killed in a prison riot. The whole thing had Qua's name written all over it, but I never asked him about it and I never will. Today was also the release of me and Kaycie's Album. It was called "Melodies from Heaven".

"You good?" My husband asked me for the millionth time that day.

"Yes, baby I'm good." I said handing him his son and kissing his lips.

Quinn walked over to me and hugged me. Her and Haz were doing well. They were in love and I was happy that Quinn had finally found a real man that could give her the love that she needed.

"I know this is still so hard for you, but I got ya back bestie and I love you so much." She said.

"I know you do, and I appreciate that best."

Italy came walking over to me and I picked her up and

kissed her little cheeks. She was getting so big and Qua had her ass spoiled rotten. Twist and Capri sat at the table with Qua's mom playing cards. Most people wouldn't consider this a happily ever after because I had lost so much and, although those losses hurt to the core, I still had a husband who adored me, beautiful healthy kids, and people who loved me enough to take this journey with me and help me through my most darkest times. I also had the music and even though Qua had yet to let go of the drug game completely at least I had him in the studio with me. His EP was coming out in a few weeks and me and my baby were headed straight to the top of the game. TOGETHER.

THE END

SUBSCRIBE

Text Shan to 22828 to stay up to date with new releases, sneak peeks, contest, and more....

SUBMISSIONS

To submit your manuscript to Shan Presents, please send the first three chapters and synopsis to submissions@shanpresents.com